THE ERRANT CHILD
WHATEVER IT TAKES

By Ozzie Logozzo

Ozzie Logozzo

Ozzie Logozzo

THE ERRANT CHILD
WHATEVER IT TAKES

MediaLinx Printing & Graphic Solutions
Vaughan

Printed in Canada by MediaLinx

MediaLinx Printing & Graphic Solutions Inc.
60 Creditview Rd., Woodbridge, ON L4L 9N4

ISBN 978-0-9948605-4-5

ACCLAIM FOR Ozzie Logozzo's

THE ERRANT CHILD
WHATEVER IT TAKES

"HOLLYWOOD MOVIE MATERIAL... This multi-level story blends, grabs and pulls you in opposing directions. Your mind is tethered and quartered by an engrossing tale that begs for a sequel."

"THE PROTAGONIST TRANSFORMED... The main character reflects Hamlet-like qualities changes into a chilling commander, still bedeviled but sure to exert exacting power and authority. One can only wish his transformation is not at the cost of his humanity."

"A DEVIL UNDISGUISED... This spoiled child in a woman's body is hot but emotionally lethal. She is enough of an obstacle and emotional turmoil to her better half without having him face perversion, crime, and betrayal, family treachery, military police and the Mafia."

"A PAGAN RELIGION CHALLENGING THE PAPACY... The inquisition ills of the Church's past broil with intrigue, corruption, malice, and avarice. A modern secret society, Stregheria, is poised to control the Papacy, discredit Roman Catholicism, and its tenets and strip Vatican City of its supremacy and wealth."

"OLD RELIGIOUS WITCHCRAFT LIVES ON... The proud legacy of the Etruscan civilization, of the Roman Empire, has persisted underground. Its revival is sure to alter the mind and spirit of individuals and society. It remains to be seen whether this anti establishment passion can correct historical wrongs or if it will pervert its own cast of characters with its own rituals and philosophy."

"FUNDAMENTALLY A LOVE STORY... This Adam and Eve, Bogart and Bacall, love story is a mercurial, artful replica of troubled marriages. Indeed, as individuals they reflect so many individual qualities gone awry: infatuation, beauty, handsomeness, prowess, jealousy, and unfaithfulness. Are we, like them, doomed to a life of dishonesty, disloyalty, and infidelity?"

"YOU WANT TO BE THE MAIN CHARACTER, BUT IT FRIGHTENS YOU... You don't want to be the beautiful damsel, but then we secretly wish we were."

"WHERE HAVE ALL THE MINOR CHARACTERS GONE... Is the author, not so secretly, setting us up for a succession of sequels? Each minor character in this novel is grist for more in-depth story telling. We have the makings of a saga."

Dedication

Writing is a beeline to rejection. To write is to endure exclusion.

For Vilma, Adam, and Kristen who fill the spaces within my heart.

Acknowledgements

My deepest appreciation to the following people, whom I have come to regard as friends, in assisting my endeavor and making this sequel possible.

Edward Barisa (Association Executive), Omar Hikaru Caum (Associate), Frank Lacaria (Printer), Michael Lacaria (Computer Specialist), Marisa Mammoliti (Graphic Designer), Tony Nardi (Actor, Playwright, Director, Producer), Michael Orlando (Artist), and a very special note of gratitude to Claudia Buscemi Prestigiacomo (Italian Translator) who provided me with thoughtful advice.

Do You Recall

Do you recall some of your childhood fantasies? I do. Playing hockey in the NHL, running the marathon, piloting a plane; skydiving, traveling around the world, becoming a movie actor, writing a best seller; and endless more flights of fancy.

These imagined experiences are a part of growing up, despite age, and greatly gratifying. I have indeed, through persistence, good fortune, and craziness, realized some of my dreams.

Where I haven't, I remain thankful of the endeavor. It is just as exhilarating in working hard and preparing for a task as it is accomplishing it. Philosophers contend that true pleasure resides in the ride not the ultimate destination. The value of a coin remains constant no matter which side you are previewing.

Approaching the half-century milestone in my professional careers, as an instructor, education administrator, a real estate broker, and executive director, I admit to a wonderful ride. In my new endeavor as an author, I appreciate all the folks I have encountered: The good, the bad, and the ugly have provided tremendous kindle for my storytelling.

THE ERRANT CHILD
WHATEVER IT TAKES

By Ozzie Logozzo

The Errant Child - Characters

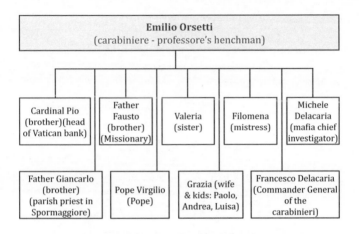

Emilio Orsetti
(carabiniere - professore's henchman)

- Cardinal Pio (brother)(head of Vatican bank)
  - Father Giancarlo (brother) (parish priest in Spormaggiore)
- Father Fausto (brother) (Missionary)
  - Pope Virgilio (Pope)
- Valeria (sister)
  - Grazia (wife & kids: Paolo, Andrea, Luisa)
- Filomena (mistress)
- Michele Delacaria (mafia chief investigator)
  - Francesco Delacaria (Commander General of the carabinieri)

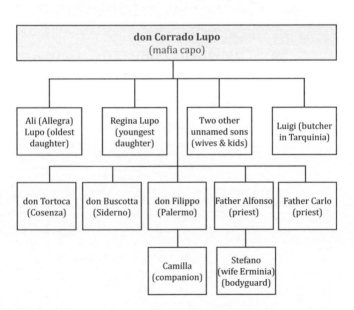

don Corrado Lupo
(mafia capo)

- Ali (Allegra) Lupo (oldest daughter)
- Regina Lupo (youngest daughter)
- Two other unnamed sons (wives & kids)
- Luigi (butcher in Tarquinia)

- don Tortoca (Cosenza)
- don Buscotta (Siderno)
- don Filippo (Palermo)
  - Camilla (companion)
- Father Alfonso (priest)
  - Stefano (wife Erminia) (bodyguard)
- Father Carlo (priest)

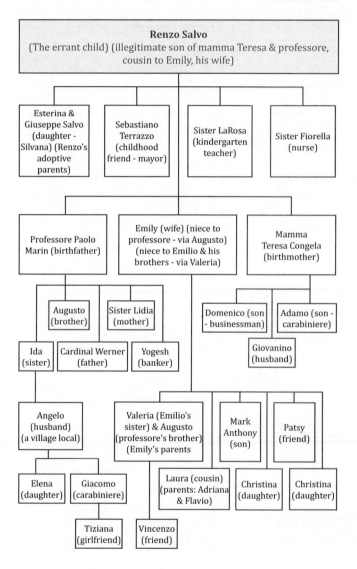

Twelve Stages

PART ONE

"Evil walks behind you."

- AC/DC

PART TWO

"This Romeo is bleeding but you can't see his blood."

- Bon Jovi

PART THREE

"I can hear him calling for my soul."

- Bob Dylan

PART FOUR

"Leave 'em burning and then you're gone."

- Abba

PART FIVE

"Holy water cannot help you now."

- Florence + the Machine

PART SIX

"There is no guidance in your kingdom."

- Thievery Corporation

PART SEVEN

"Don't get too close. It's dark inside. It's where my demons hide."

- Imagine Dragons

PART EIGHT

"There will be an answer, let it be."

- Paul McCartney

PART NINE

"Don't stop thinking about tomorrow."

- Fleetwood Mac

PART TEN

"I know, it's everybody's sin, you gotta lose to know how to win."

- Aerosmith

PART ELEVEN

"There's a killer on the road."

- The Doors

PART TWELVE

"The first cut is the deepest."

- Rod Stewart

PART ONE

"Evil walks behind you." - AC/DC

Chapter 1

Buenos Aires, Argentina

Celebrations aside, tomorrow's day of reckoning is today.

A sea of exuberant spectators overflows the *barrios* of downtown Buenos Aires watching carnival crazies in colorful costumes screech loud-mouth vulgarities. Other audacious performers parade in an extravagance of frivolity and narcissistic madness. The entire city is alight pulsating with steel-pan sounds. There's an earthquake of revelry, chanting and bellowing - it's party time. There is no escaping the hustle and bustle of the festivities.

The *Murgas*, street musicians, march the streets. Dancers with sky-high headdresses frolic to the tunes of percussion instruments.

Cymbals clash in sync with flashing boobs. Deafening drumbeats shake stomachs and wiggle inside feelings. Fireworks crackle and illuminate the night sky with a kaleidoscope of colors and designs. Hundreds of green, gold, blue, red, yellow and white bursts of light shoot onto the black sky and rain down in fizzled oblivion.

The high dynamism of national spirit unchains curbed emotions and impulses. Celebrants consume alcohol with abandon and release behavior best suited to an insane asylum.

A very pretty woman with thick brown-black hair curling down her slender figure is choreographing her way home, after grocery shopping, through the unabashed carousers. She is happy and excited swinging her satchel like a pendulum. She holds her head high, smiling and laughing at the hoopla that encircles her. She is ablaze with energy and eager to get home to her man.

Twenty paces behind her, a short, squatty man with a white fedora is profusely perspiring through his white linen sports coat as he shadows and tracks the woman's footsteps.

A half-inebriated partygoer recognizes the passing beauty and calls out to her.

"Tiziana, over here. Where are you going? Come drink with us. Where is Giacomo?"

Tiziana notices him and several other shared friends and madly waves at them.

"Hi Antonio. Give me time to bring these groceries home. Giacomo and I will come out shortly. Don't black out. Save us some."

In unison, the friends raise their bottles and shout.

"We'll drink to that!"

Tiziana is carrying a cotton grocery bag much too small for the oversized, spicy, herbed *empanada*, stuffed bread, and medley of leafy greens that spill over the small sack. She carries the bag deftly; dodging flying streamers, oversized balloons, flailing arms, dancing feet, discarded beer bottles and even wild and witless merrymakers engaged in foam fights.

The squatty stalker remains still, unaffected by the infectious beats and rhythms of marching bands and dancers. The cacophony of pulsating sounds mishmash around him but he resolutely eyes his target's treasures: her flawless skin, her long legs, and her figure-hugging elegant, lace, mini dress, but especially her energetic, passionate pace. The woman is simply drop dead gorgeous though a bit too bony for his taste. His gaze is practically glued to her *samba* swinging ass.

The man is grateful for the hundreds of *murgas* and *mirgueros* around him who are beating the oversized drums and cymbals. The pumping beats along with deafening chants from the multitude are enough to burst eardrums. It is just the kind of uproar and chaos needed to cover up an assassination.

The hunted and hunter meander through the rabble rousers who are clad in exotic, colorful costumes of sequins and feathers that festoon the extravaganza. It's carnival time and with it comes all the bizarre tastes and outrageous looks. Intricate vibrant costumes co-mingle with assorted stages of undress. Nipple tape, speedos, thongs exposing tanned buns, and other risqué wear that barely mask the naughty bits appear to subscribe to the one universal law of the pompadour parade: Make it sexy; Make it tight; and Make it freakishly delight.

With a last-minute sprint through the jubilant horde, the woman reaches her front doorstep at the corner of *Avenida Independencia* and *Santiago del Estero*. Giacomo's motorcycle is parked on the sidewalk next to a leafless, diseased and dying tree. The apartment complex is a tall and narrow seven-story dirty red brick structure with concrete balconies. It is sandwiched between a white stucco, four-story mixed-use building and a single-story retail variety outlet. The entire *barrio*, as far as the eye can see, has been developed *à la carte*. There is no rhyme or reason or discernible urban planning strategy. Laundromats, drugstores, auto body shops, family restaurants, clothing stores, electronic repair, and jewelry boutiques share real estate with low and high-rise apartment buildings. Two common elements string together all this diversity. Everywhere, there is clutter and littered trash, including discarded condoms. Everywhere, windows and doors are protected behind steel bars.

Tiziana's residence is barred by a wrought iron gated façade, spanning ground-level to the underside of the first balcony, protecting an interior small flight of steps leading to a wooden entry door. She slides her key in and unlocks the heavy steel gate. She skips up the steps readied with yet another key to enter within.

The stranger is quick enough to insert a holiday flyer against the lock's strike plate preventing the bolt from entering the doorjamb. Although the gate closes with its characteristic metallic clank, the spring-loaded bolt does not engage.

Seconds after Tiziana enters her home, the stranger slips in. At the windowless wooden door, he uses a jagged rake, lock pick, to effortlessly enter unannounced. He stands silently inside. He hears voices down the hallway.

"Giacomo, what are you doing? You're not even dressed yet? *Muoviti!* Hurry up!"

The bedroom balcony sliding door is open. The *fiesta* pandemonium resonates throughout the suite stunningly decorated by what can only be a woman's touch. Giacomo, with all the carefreeness one would find in a gym locker room, is sitting on the tufted bench at the end of the bed surfing the Net on his iPad. He is clean-shaven, muscular and wearing only slim-fit boxer briefs. The stretchy knit fabric accentuates his machismo, particularly as he stands to embrace Tiziana seconds after she deposits the bag of groceries on the soft area rug. She obliges by jumping and wrapping her legs around his hips. They kiss and dance wildly.

They pirouette back to where they started. There, Giacomo gently lowers his lover onto the edge of the bed. She sits legs spread eagle, reaching up to rummage his hair with both hands as he bends over to kiss her neck, one hand on her breast and the other on her crotch. Unable to resist any longer, he removes her blouse and she unclips her bra. There is a moment of mutual observation. He glares. She giggles. Wickedly, she grasps his boxer briefs and pulls them down to his knees. Only one word escapes her as she sees her prize.

"Wow!"

"Nice ass, too," announces the intruder.

The couple is startled. The street stranger is standing with his shoulder against the edge of the doorframe, hat in hand.

Giacomo is dumbstruck with fearful

recognition. Tiziana sneers at the man as she cowers behind Giacomo's physique.

"Oh, my God. Who the fuck are you? Get out of my house!" shouts Tiziana.

"Don't you read your bible? It is disgraceful for a woman to speak out in a congregation. This is a congregation so shut the fuck up. You've already pissed me off."

Giacomo maneuvers to pull up his briefs but no one is interested in modesty, least of all Tiziana. She sees a pair of scissors resting beside the portable sewing machine in front of the bedroom window. Animated, she stands, with frontal exposure and shouts at the stranger.

"Get the fuck out of my house, now!"

The stranger pulls his pistol from behind his fedora and shoots Tiziana through the side of her face as she lunges for the scissors.

"What a shameful, disgraceful bitch. That's who you left the family for?"

"Uncle, please. Please, uncle!"

Giacomo kneels and looks down at Tiziana in a pool of blood. The bullet appears to have entered the side of her skull and travelled through the entire length of her face, out the other side and lodged itself in the back wall next to the window frame.

Emilio advances toward Giacomo, step by step, speaking slowly.

"Uncle? That's how you greet me? You

cry uncle. You don't address me with honor and respect?"

"Zio Emilio, I'm sorry. You caught me by surprise. I do respect you."

Giacomo is shaking like a playful jelly toy.

Emilio, consumed by anger, forces his gun barrel into Giacomo's mouth breaking several teeth.

"I made you *Comandante*. I made you powerful. I put my reputation on the line. And, what do you do? You fraternize with mobsters. Scheme against *La Stregheria* and the Society of Twin Winged-Horses. You flee the country with a Mafia princess."

Every blood vessel in Emilio's face is bursting. His eyes are reddening. Blood drips from his nose. He is on the verge of a stroke.

"You betrayed me. Me! Me! You betrayed my trust."

Emilio fires the gun. The bullet splatters skull and brain matter on the bedsheets. Blood sprays the high headboard.

Methodically, Emilio plants his revolver in Giacomo's lifeless hand. He takes his time removing and pocketing his surgical gloves. There is no worry of detection from nosy neighbors. The carnival's hullabaloo continues to break sound barriers. Over the next few days, the bodies will decompose undisturbed until the macabre stench invites an investigation.

Emilio's anxiety, anger, sadness, frustration and even grief subside only to be replaced by an emotion he rarely experiences: fear. Having to now travel to the United States as Renzo Salvo's envoy to deliver *La Stregheria's* message to representatives of the five crime families in New York City evokes unaccustomed fear. Emilio exits, dabbing his brow with the sleeve of his jacket.

PART TWO

"This Romeo is bleeding but you can't see his blood."
– Bon Jovi

Chapter 2

Tarquinia, central Italy

Ali and Regina loiter under the balmy evening sky in front of the *municipal* building and fountain waiting for Renzo. Ali had graciously accepted Renzo's dinner invitation after their early afternoon encounter, last week, in *Piazza Cavour*. Regina, feeling like the third wheel, tries to beg off but Ali insists she stays. She is desperately trying to distract her younger sister from obsessing over their parents' death.

"Good evening ladies. You must be tired and hungry from your touristic adventures throughout Tuscany," Renzo says as he approaches.

Regina notices that Renzo has emerged from the *carabinieri* stationhouse. She despises the *carabinieri* for killing her family.

Ali greets Renzo with kisses on both cheeks with a light brush of her lips against his.

Regina is wedded to her androgynous, Goth appearance. Even her perfume is musky and masculine. In contrast, Ali, with high heels, cream-colored skinny jeans and a tucked-in burgundy blouse, looks smashing and smells spicy. Renzo carries himself well in black denim and a V-neck summer sweater.

Ali wraps her arm inside of Renzo's as they walk the short distance along *via San Giuseppe* to *via Menotti Garibaldi* to his favorite wine bar, *Grotta Estrusca*.

The restaurant, essentially a cavern, features all the best local vintages of wine, bountifully displayed, and offers excellent food. The dark varnished wood floors, brick walls, massive wine barrels and secluded dimly lit tables give a casual, cozy and romantic feeling. Patrons keep to themselves but offer warm welcome smiles. The waiter offers the threesome a table in a quiet corner.

"We are staying in *Civitavecchia* continuing to take side tours to *Firenze, Pisa, Cinque Terre* and, of course, *Tarquinia*. After the death of our parents, I am trying to persuade my younger sister to come live with me in America," says Ali.

Taking a seat opposite Renzo, Regina reacts emphatically.

"I am not going anywhere. I have unfinished business here," vows Regina.

Renzo ignores the emotional eruption. Ali looks irritated.

"If it's okay, after dinner, I would like to drive you back to your hotel. Taxis are scarce and expensive."

"We'd like that, right Regina?"

Regina remains silent. Renzo has difficulty assessing her quietness to be thoughtfulness or rebelliousness. He feels her long, fixed, cold stare.

Ali breaks the darkening mood.

"Last week, you mentioned that your glamorous wife and children have gone back home without you. What's that all about?" asks Ali.

Ali is succinct and straightforward. Her attentiveness has gone beyond infatuation.

"It's a long story for another time," bemoans Renzo. He redirects the conversation.

"I'm told that your father was Corrado Lupo. I have been informed of the destruction and deaths that have occurred in *Gioiosa*. I feel horrible. I'm sorry for your loss. Please accept my deepest condolences," says Renzo looking first at Regina and then at Ali.

The waiter has returned to serve water. Ali leans forward to whisper.

"Thank you. Unfortunately, my family wasn't saintly. I left for America because my father and I had very divergent philosophies on life. I detested his business dealings," murmurs Ali while looking at Regina.

The waiter leaves allowing Ali to resume a normal speaking volume. She directs her comments to Renzo.

"In the end, I hated my father. Regina fails to understand but that's also, as you say, a long story for another time. I have no grief for my dead parents. Actually, I feel relief."

Regina refuses to look at Ali. She gazes vacantly at her black polished fingernails.

"Renzo, what about you? Aren't you going back home?" questions Ali.

Renzo ponders before giving a pleasant answer tinged with sadness.

"No, I'm not. I have decided to stay in *Tarquinia*. I have accepted a post with the *carabinieri*."

Regina looks at Renzo. If looks could kill, Renzo would be dead.

Chapter 3

Civitavecchia, central Italy

The drive to *Civitavecchia* is unsettling. Try as I may, I am not able to bond with Regina. She just doesn't like me. Her body language and expressions challenge me. I suspect she blames the *carabinieri* and me, by association, for the tragedy of her parents.

Ali, as well, agitates me with her ability to uncap my deepest self. She seems to undress my mind down to stark nakedness with her trusting persona and kindhearted words. I feel the unity of our thoughts, making love, before our bodies even touch.

"Renzo, please come up for a drink. *Affogato al caffè corretto* is my specialty. I have limited culinary prowess but I love the mixture of ice-cream, amaretto and coffee. It's simple to make."

Ali is factual not apologetic. I am not surprised. The image of Ali as a homemaker and traditional cook strains my imagination.

I lick my lips, realize the sexual innuendo, and bite my lip to hide my embarrassment.

"I know the drink well. It is a coffee-based dessert: espresso poured over a scoop of ice cream with a *grappa* or brandy shot usually added." I say, feeling stupidly pedantic.

Regina disapproves but Ali giggles and pulls me by the arm before I have any thought of disappearing.

The Hotel Miramare is located on the seafront with its pleasant beach and boardwalk and is small and elegant. The women have separate rooms with balconies and an enchanting view of the sea. Regina opts to ostracize herself and, unceremoniously, locks herself in her room. Ali pulls me into her neighboring small suite. While I admire the view of the port and the several docked cruise liners through the open doors and fluttering drapes, Ali fusses over her promised cocktail concoction on the kitchenette counter.

I find myself on a path in which there is no turning back. I have severed ties with Emily, my adulterous spouse. Yes, I have provided trust monies for my two children but I have abandoned them as well. However, engrossed in their selfishness, it may be years before my children sense any sorrow for their errant father.

By virtue of birth, I have taken the reigns of a secret society, *La Stregheria*, that controls Vatican

City and its papal puppet. I wage war against the Mafia network that promulgates a culture of death in its earnest endeavors to control illegal, lucrative activities. I lead a quasi-autonomous, military sect of the *Carabinieri*, whose moral imperatives are idealistic, perhaps perilous. I am astride two stallions pulling my chariot in opposing directions. I fear my choices and decisions and my own descent into Hell. Is this my destiny?

Ali brings our beverages with a smile and a kiss on my cheek. I return the smile in wonderment. The coffee's aroma, smoky and nutty, arouses my mind. This woman is the opposite of Emily. Is she my preordained soul mate? I can't help but stare in her eyes.

"So, when is the last time you had sex?" says Ali while teasing out a strand of curls in her hair.

Ali's bravado is more of her boundless energy, not simply impetuousness. She has a knack for wielding mental and muscle imbalances in me. I gulp.

"Not having it is my new normal," I confess.

I can't think of what else to say. I'm not so much flushed by her blunt directness than resigned to a changed reality.

"So, it's not a simple rut? You do realize that you can get sick, or even die, if you suffer a sexless state? Your self-esteem needs orgasms," says Ali slyly humorous but serious.

Ali makes me smile.

"I've never heard it stated that way. Is that a pick-up line?" I reply fumbling for words.

She takes the cup from my hands and places

it on the window sill next to hers.

"It's a jump up line," says Ali with widening eyes as I look on with a confused look.

Suddenly, she jumps on me with legs open dropping us both on the couch upending a small vase of vibrant Tuscan poppies, scattering gorgeous rose colored papery petals on the floor.

"You're such a tight-ass. You need sexercising. I'm going to give you a treat to purge you of your rigidity."

Pinned against the sofa, her whispered words send shivers down my spine.

Ali kisses me gently. First my lips. Then, my ears. Our eye contact and body-to-body contact is intense. She begins to disrobe me. As she unbuckles my pants, she smirks.

"I want to taste you."

The tension and heat put me over the edge. I reverse our positions, stripping her of her clothes. Naked, we twist and twirl in tantric love.

It is tantalizing to be on top. Her tilted head and cocked chin speak of her sensuousness.

I think I hear a noise behind me like a mouse scurrying across the floor.

"Did you hear something?"

Ali's eyes, opened wide like an owl, peers over my shoulder.

"What are you doing there? Get lost!"

I turn and fumble to grab a toss cushion. I see Regina's eyes retreat and fade into the darkness.

PART THREE

"I can hear him calling for my soul." – Bob Dylan

Chapter 4

Palermo, Sicily

Hooked by a seemingly incredible story from his compatriot, Father Alfonso asks that they scout a place to sit and talk further. Father Carlo is the new priest for the neighboring church, *Parrocchia San Nicolo di Bari All'Albergheria*, a stone's throw away from Father Alfonso's *Chiesa del Gesù*. Father Carlo is happy to return to Palermo. He was born on a side street, *via del Bosco*, that intersects *via Ballarò*—the street that houses the city's oldest marketplace.

At first, Father Alfonso smirked at what he thought was a recounting of the danger of surrendering to a woman's struggle during a confessional. Now he realizes that Father Carlo is not troubled about breaking his vow of celibacy and possibly facing perdition. Rather, Father Carlo is mortified by the woman's tale told during his stay in *Trento*. A distraught, suicidal mother, had confessed to him her participation in the death of her dying son. Her family needed money. Her son was dying of cancer. She did not want him to suffer the same agonizing death as her husband.

Grabbing two bananas from a fruit stand without payment under the sentry of an offended middle-age saleslady in a soiled apron, Father Alfonso suggests they take a seat on two empty food crates beside the vendor's shop.

"Tell me more about this woman and her son. What did you mean she needed money, yet her son drove a *Professore's Alfa Romeo* sport car?" probes Father Alfonso.

"Alfonso, you're missing the point. This woman wants to kill herself. Maybe she already has."

Father Carlo is exasperated but continues his tale.

"The *Professore*, leaving *Spormaggiore*, apparently needed a driver to transport his car to the University in Trento because he had to take a flight to Rome. The woman gave me the impression that she knew the fatal car accident her son was involved in was going to happen."

Father Carlo clasps his hands in prayer.

"I suspect she and the *Professore* planned it," says Father Carlo making the sign of the cross.

Father Carlo's compassion is convincing. He closes his eyes, clenches his fists and slowly shakes his head from side to side. His agony is undisputable.

Father Alfonso does not reciprocate his

friend's feelings. He is on the verge of rage realizing that the *Professore* is still alive.

"Carlo, the woman is obviously in a state of depression. I don't think she is confessing to a heinous crime. You did not withhold absolution. Aptly, you recommended she visit her family physician and you outlined the required repentance. Don't let your imagination run rampant. You can't do anything more. Regardless, a confession is sacred. The seal of confession is absolute."

The priests peel and eat their bananas in silence. The picturesque, open-air, farmer's market is a mecca of social interaction between vendors and customers. It spreads across several blocks within the historic center of Palermo. There are permanent stores and massive stalls displaying a wide assortment of dry goods, souvenirs, artifacts and foodstuff. The mood is merry. The clatter of conversations is cheery. The entire spectrum of rainbow colors adorns the homes, canopies, clothing and goods for sale. The language is replete with give-and-take bargaining over prices.

The only sour note in the market belongs to Father Alfonso.

"Carlo, there is nothing more scandalous than a parishioner who shows no loyalty and respect for his family or spiritual life. We are but shepherds caring for our sheep. We cannot save all of them. As ambassadors of Christ, we are taught to shun such men as this *Professore* you describe."

Father Alfonso's demeanor turns menacing.

"Sometimes, impious thoughts of vengeance and retribution succumb me. I yearn to cleanse the flock and rule with an iron fist," declares Father Alfonso.

Father Carlo is taken aback by his colleague's outburst.

"Alfonso, you are a man of the cloth, not a Mafioso."

It is beginning to drizzle. Father Alfonso looks at his friend with a renewed mask of sanity and charm.

"Father Carlo, *Per l'amor di Dio* (For the love of God). I believe in justice. To know me is to know that I am a gentle and mild man. I wouldn't harm a fly."

Chapter 5

Palermo, Sicily

Rainy days turn the Forum Palermo Shopping Mall into an ideal meeting place for Mafia strategists. There is a high volume of shoppers. No one pays attention to others who aren't in their immediate walking path.

From the inside, the mall belies the moniker that Sicily is a city of contrasts. The mall is modern with a complex of abutting stores along interconnecting walkways. There are large department retailers, stand-alone stores, food courts, and other attractions such as movie theaters geared to turn the mall into a leisure facility. Without peeking outside, you could not discern if you were situated in Toronto, Montreal, Los Angeles or New York City. Certainly, the average tourist would be surprised to learn that just outside this mall lies Mafia-infested Palermo. The mall serves as an oft-times meeting place. Petty ante criminals use the food court tables to idle away daylight by playing cards while touching base on upcoming nocturnal shenanigans.

Don Filippo prefers a small coffee shop with some tables located at the base of an escalator. He is sitting at a small table with his back to the wall. Don Filippo savors his brioche with jam while waiting for his *cappuccino* to cool.

Father Alfonso is at the counter where the *barista* offers up a double *espresso macchiato* with a dark chocolate square. Casually, he joins Don Filippo at the table.

"Our presence in Sicilian life and the very order of our business enterprises are threatened. We are a wounded octopus, bleeding from every pore rather than sucking in our rightful claims. The government continues to exert its power by dismembering our networks. We need to demonstrate that the Mafia is a mighty force not folklore. The *carabinieri* and the Church's puppets will succeed if we remain resting," implores Father Alfonso.

"Father Alfonso, you have a flair for the dramatic. We Sicilians are not sleeping, only strategizing. Renzo, the bastard son, knows he is a marked man. He knows he will be killed. He just doesn't know when and how," says don Filippo nonchalantly.

"Don Filippo, it's time for action. You must exert your leadership. The *Professore* used the military power of the *carabinieri* against us. We fought back fire with fire but Renzo is using the authority and wealth of the Church against us. The Pope is courting the common people with community and social programs. They are trying to make us irrelevant," insists Father Alfonso.

"Father, let's walk. It's safer," says don Filippo looking about for eavesdroppers.

Father Alfonso, in priestly garb, and Don Filippo, dapper and brooding, walk along the corridors away from potential eavesdroppers.

"We have killed a lot of policemen. We can't continue to directly battle the government without further repercussion. We can't afford to have any more investigations into our banking and financial records that was the core of the *Professore's* stratagem that took us down. We cannot afford to cut off dealings with our German bank."

Father Alfonso grips don Filippo's arm, drawing him closer to his whispering.

"Don Filippo, the *Professore* is alive."

Don Filippo looks at the priest without missing a step but his face reddens with the onslaught of blood that rushes to his clenched jaw. Don Filippo doesn't question the veracity of the statement. He values his messenger's talent for knowing.

"My source is unassailable," utters Father Alfonso with conviction.

"This news presents many complications. I doubted the son's powers to unite the forces of the military police and the church. But, the father is still alive. This could be crippling to us if we don't act," says don Filippo.

A moment of silence is followed by a directive.

"Father, call a meeting of the *capifamiglia* (family bosses) for St. Joseph's Day at the Grand Hotel Et Des Palmes. We need their passive cooperation before we act."

Looking Father Alfonso squarely in his eyes, don Filippo's command is clear.

"Find him. Kill him. This time, no slipups."

PART FOUR

"Leave 'em burning and then you're gone." - Abba

Chapter 6

Toronto, Canada

"No, it's horrible. That asshole. I'm tired of sulking on the couch with my meddlesome mother driving me insane," seethes Emily.

"Two cinnamon dolce Frappuccino for Emily," barks the pimple-faced, Starbucks barista.

"I'll get them," says Patty cheerfully.

....

I watch Patty spring towards the counter collecting our late afternoon fix. I like Patty. She's fit, smart, and my soulmate. She mirrors my outlook and tastes. She is my lightning rod but her criticism is always conveyed constructively. Patty is blessed with a partner who is tall, handsome, professional and affluent; who is emotionally secure and philosophically relaxed. Their open relationship allows for indulgences, not the restricted monogamous, committed crap preached by Renzo.

To sip a cappuccino after lunch is a gastrointestinal desecration in Italy. Americans are more business minded and ignorant of such affectations. In matters of food and drink, Italians are obsessed with visceral sensitivities. I must admit that Italian men are my weakness, not the sad replicas that exist here.

Since unceremoniously returning from *la bella* Italia, cast aside from my prick of a spouse, I fantasize about an olive skin, clean-shaven, lavender–scented Italian man with hard-muscled abs. His torso, thighs, and calves clothed only in a full-length *cappuccio* (hood) staring at me with dark, brown eyes as I squirm naked beneath silky-soft, satin sheets surrounded by an excess of colorful candles. It's very different from the sad, self-indulgent scene I act out most days with Patty, my best friend, or Marisa, my 'you are not running late, you are rude and selfish' other best friend.

The Starbucks regulars who sip their spiced lattes and other concoctions, accepting of the prestigious, steep prices for basic java, are the in-crowd. Or so they think. Like an infestation of parasites, the obnoxious sit and chatter for want of attention while freeloaders with empty cups huddle for hours over their books and computers infused with unreliable Wi-Fi waves. Dudes and trend-setters come and go while real estate agents sit and expose pictures, feature sheets, and financial spreadsheets that detail veiled ultimatums to their clients. Then, there are the quiet, lonely males or females who hang out just to feel a sense of belonging amongst the transient group. These squatters lack love—perhaps a knife to commit harry carry. The endless line of customers that snakes its way from the door to the counter is revealing. From average to aficionado, from student to businessperson, this caffeine-addicted sampling of our greater society flocks like bees to honey. It's our version of the *piazza* phenomenon of Europe.

"I think your mom really cares about you," says Patty returning with the coffees.

"My mother doesn't give a shit. I told her to stop speaking to me. It's been over six months and we've barely spoken more than simple sentences," laments Emily.

"Emily, I feel bad for your mom. She just wants what's best for you. And, what the hell did you do to your upper lip? Did you get Botox?"

I ignore Patty's precise presumption.

"I'm Googling New York city flights. I need to get away. Marisa said she would tag along for the next long weekend. Her husband spends more time at his laundry business than he does at home. Are you interested in coming? We would all have a fucking blast."

"My hubby wouldn't object but is ditching your mom wise?" asks Patty.

My expression communicates disgust, but I don't give a damn.

"I don't care. She'll survive," I proclaim.

I notice the real estate agent in his hilariously

hideous, eye-popping three-piece suit. It's summer's final surge of heat. What is he thinking? He is mugging me with greater intensity than his clammy, checkered brown wardrobe. He rouses my contempt. I mouth 'what a dick' in his direction. With smugness, he flips me the bird and leaves.

"You're going to get yourself in real trouble one day with that attitude of yours," warns Patty

I can't contain my laughter.

"Stop mothering me. Are you coming to New York or not, Patty?"

"Yes, Ms. Danger Seeker. As long as I don't have to cart you back home in a body bag," says Patty in all seriousness.

Chapter 7

Toronto, Canada

"Frank dropped by the store today. I think he's still interested in you."

Ignoring Emma's conclusion, I respond to my store clerk without emotion.

"Yeah, he texted me. He was going to an after-office party and wanted me to tag along. I told him to have a drink on me and that I would share a coffee with him in the morning while he nursed his hangover."

"Isn't he still married, with kids?" probes Emma.

"He's only being playful. He doesn't get much attention at home. I don't think he's had sex for months," I bluntly reply.

Emma giggles. I smirk at my thought of having speared my mother's traditional values just a bit.

"Your mom is in the storage room, finishing inventory."

"Thanks Emma. It's ten minutes to closing. I'll finish locking up. I'll see you in the morning. You look smashing. Big date?"

Emma nods and smiles blushing.

"Do what I would do. It's fun and satisfying," I tease.

Emma gives me a confirming chuckle and escapes in earnest.

I dread facing my mother. Her looks are endless, masterful expressions of guilt and pity. I busy myself replacing misplaced fabrics and stray garments, double-checking, detailing and ensure nothing shelved gets wrinkled. My trendy clothing boutique has prospered. I pay rent to myself now that I own the building which includes Frank's law office next door. He discounted his fee for processing and registering my divorce papers.

I see my mother emerge from the backroom. She is the epitome of the life-long seamstress having learned exceptional sewing skills at an early age. She has an unnerving eye for color and detail as well as a sixth sense for discerning people's underlying thoughts and wants.

"Do you know where Christina is? She's out with that boy-crazy crowd; the girls wear slutty clothes, have delinquent morals and gossip about everyone. She doesn't have a male role model anymore now that Mark Anthony is off studying in

England. I'm worried about her."

My mother shares her genuine concern for Christina but her focused glare suggests, 'what's a woman without a man?' I am tempted to spout, 'free to enjoy all men!'

"She'll be fine. She has you for sound, sensible, protective advice," I say unable to mask my disrespect.

Demoralized, mom grunts desperation.

Mustering bravado, I state my intentions.

"I'm going to New York City for the long weekend with my girlfriends."

My mother looks at me as if I squashed her soul.

"You're doing this to spite me, right? Just because I wouldn't let you go with your reckless friends to Punta Cana or to the cottage with those drunkards while you were single. Every chance you get, you run away."

"Holy shit mom. How often are you going to bring up that crap?"

I feel like punching her in the face. I remember my teenage years being awash with tantrums and tears.

"You still don't understand! I am worried. I am just looking out for you. You were too young and foolish to understand. Your hormones were out of control. I hid your passport so you wouldn't do anything you'd regret the rest of your life. And, I don't mean just getting drunk or inviting your friends to the house for a drinking party or shoplifting at Walmart."

I refuse to engage. I'm exhausted from

memories of my fucked-up youth.

"You think I don't know that you tried to pick the lock on my jewelry cabinet to see if your passport was in there. I knew you had put a down payment on the trip and that you had booked a flight. My God, I remember how your dad would get so angry. It crazed him to know that you were lying to him. For him to think he was losing you. In the end, he couldn't take it. I think that's why he left us for a while."

Her guilt trip is boundless.

"I fucked up many more times than you can even imagine," I say wanting to hurt her.

That shut her up. No doubt she's wondering what other calamity she missed out on.

As a teenager, I remember thinking how I could kill my dad. How I even wanted to kill myself. I ran away once and stayed at Marisa's house for two nights. I didn't care about getting into trouble. It beat staying home and being bored. I was so confused. I still am.

My mother looks at me teary-eyed. Her voice is soft and broken.

"Renzo is a good man. He truly loves you. He is so much like your father, respectful and honorable. The divorce papers wouldn't mean anything to him. He would take you back in a heartbeat. Don't give up on him. I can take care of everything here. Go back to Italy. Get him back."

My mother's words evoke painful, regretful memories. Lately, I feel dumb and numb; that I shouldn't be doing what I'm doing but that it's too late. Renzo has moved on. It's too late, isn't it?

Chapter 8

Broadway, New York City

There is something very alluring about Sapphire. She is singularly focused on making fantasies come true for men, for a price. For this, she needs a stacked stable of escorts: exquisite, starlet, perfectly coiffed, glamorous and cultivated purebreds.

Sapphire, precocious and clever, knows her stock of females. She values whites, chestnuts and blacks that she is able to shape into exotic gemstones. It is not enough to simply be perfumed, pretty and appropriately dressed. A high-priced escort's true value resides in polishing: a proper education in feminine etiquette and knowledge of men's sexual needs and desires.

Going to *Freemans*, a restaurant in Manhattan, after attending a production at *The Box* has paid off handsomely in the past. The eatery swarms with potential sex workers who continue to flaunt their wares. They go there to balance their blood-alcohol concentration with cups of coffee. Sapphire is expecting the same payoff tonight.

Meanwhile at the theater, thrill seekers and some noticeable movie and music celebrities are treated to an outrageous, explicit cabaret of naked acrobats, hardcore strippers and lewd singers. Blaring music mixed with copious, ridiculously-priced drinks has intensified the scandalous obscenity. Amongst the cacophony and the chaos, Sapphire notices three attractive women unwinding with each decadent performance in the risqué burlesque.

The theater and the neighborhood alike encourage guests to dress stylishly...which means scantily. Sapphire, with her flaming red hair and eyelids saturated by shades of blue, wears a two-toned mini leather dress with stretch side panels and a zip-up front. Knowing that men are visual creatures, Sapphire's targeted ladies have equally dressed to attract. Their outfits could best be described as racy erotica. All three teeter in black patent sky-scraping stiletto heels. Their lips pout with scarlet red lipstick. Their eyes are adorned with long lashes.

One of the women, 'Marisa' embossed on her clutch purse, is dressed in a red, off-the-shoulder, short-sleeved blouse with a billowing bodice merging into a seamed at the side, fitted skirt with a mini, straight hemline. The second woman, our lady in white, wears an ultra-short party dress with a plunging cowl neck. Her breasts spill out. The third woman, clad black as a raven, inspires the most curiosity in Sapphire. This blond beauty, called Emily by her girlfriends, wears a sexy mini dress with a halter neckline. The lightly transparent fabric glitters. The outline of her black, low rise G-string is subtle but detectable. This particular beauty engrosses Sapphire not so much by what she is wearing but by her poise and self-assurance. Unlike the exaggerated makeup of her companions, she does not broadcast fake high maintenance.

After the curtain call, Sapphire followed the trio to *Freemans* as anticipated, a restaurant on the Lower East Side. With its rustic and colonial décor, this hidden-away, old-world tavern incredulously draws a hip crowd. The pseudo escorts. The wannabee ladies of the night. Inside, the atmosphere is haughty and abnormal with prices to match.

Emily and her friends sit along the right side of the horseshoe-shaped bar sharing bitter black coffees and wedges of rich, dense, iconic New York cheesecake. Sapphire, businesswoman and hustler, approaches the women. She greets them with the same relaxed conviviality that characterizes women chattering in restrooms. The exchange is neighborly and jovial.

In the course of their conversation that jumps from fashion to drinks to the daring production at *The Box* theater, Sapphire learns Marisa and Patty are helping Emily celebrate her divorce. While some may think it bad taste, Sapphire empathizes with the women's need to embrace reality and party. Emily surprises her friends by saying that she is considering moving to New York. In unison, Marisa and Patty's mood shifts as they suddenly are reminded of home, family and work responsibilities.

Sapphire appears happy but fusses as she prepares to leave for another engagement. Uncharacteristically, she fumbles through her purse and plants a hundred-dollar bill on the counter.

"Ladies I'm late for an appointment," says Sapphire.

She's flustered but recoups.

"Ladies, it was entirely my pleasure. The drinks and dessert are on me," says Sapphire apologetically.

Emily notices a Louis Vuitton canvas cardholder on the bar counter. Surmising it belongs to Sapphire, she picks it up and rushes to return it to its rightful owner. She catches up with Sapphire just outside the restaurant entrance.

"Sapphire, wait. You forgot this."

Sapphire turns and looks at Emily with a cryptic, intense smile.

"I left it there for you. Call me."

Sapphire beams and walks out of the light and into the back of a black limousine.

Emily draws a single business card from inside the card holder. It is all black with white calligraphy. Along with the phone number it reads, *Sapphire, Supreme Escort Services, Favor a flirtatious life*.

Chapter 9

Greenwich Village, New York City

Sapphire and I sprint, under heavy rain, for the coffee shop across the street eager for a robust boost to celebrate our run of good fortune. Java Joe, I doubt that Joe is even his real name, gets more and more frisky with his comments the more we frequent the joint. He's a bit of an asshole but the robust brew is to die for.

"Hey girls, welcome back. You must be coming from the gym. Did you spin? Your bodies look good enough to eat. I could dip you in chocolate and dive in if I hadn't partied so much on the weekend."

I know our gym clothes are doing the talking. Sapphire and I look like we're in a relationship with our matching red hoodies, black leggings, and white runners. Our next-to-nothing leggings let our buttocks bob freely with every movement. Sapphire decides to play ball while I just roll my eyes, fluttering my eyelashes.

"All those women must have tired you out. Do you need a nap?" jokes Sapphire.

Joe doesn't quite get it.

"Yeah. No. Listen up, there's a party every Friday and Saturday. It's routine. You girls should come along for the ride. There's something there for everyone, weirdos and virgins," says Joe shifting his eyes from Sapphire to me.

I loathe that he accentuates his statement with a final locked glance at my crotch.

Sapphire remains standoffish and superior.

"Emily and I will take you up on it if we are ever desperate. For now, bring us our usual."

"You bet, black and beautiful."

The barista slips behind the massive espresso machine.

"Don't let him unnerve you. He's been trying to get into my pants for years. His pitch never changes. That fake, spray tan looks shitty. I'd rather bang an albino. But ignore him. I've got a gift for you," beams Sapphire.

"For me? Really? What is it?"

"Come on. Let's sit by the window. I love the look and sound of the rain."

Seated and comfy, Sapphire presents me with two airline tickets to Amsterdam. I am thrilled.

"Wow. Why?"

"Consider it an anniversary gift. We've been, you know, together six months and we've made loads of cash. It's time we took a break from escorting and self-indulge. We both need a vacation."

Java Joe interrupts my thoughts by placing two chai lattes on the small square table.

"Airline tickets? Is there one for me? I could carry your belongings by day and serve as your sex slave at night. I'm well-equipped to serve you both. I do think there is some black blood in my ancestry."

Sapphire grins at him and swats his behind to usher him away.

"I can't wait. It will be the perfect pick-me-up after I visit Christina, in Troy, tomorrow."

"What's the name of that boarding school again?"

"Emma Willard."

"How is your daughter doing?"

"She hated it at first. An all-girls school. A curriculum geared to empowering women. No boys. Now, I think she'll end up running the school. She's a natural leader and a pain in everybody's butt."

"Ah, my kind of woman."

"It's me again, ladies. I brought you both *cannoli siciliani* filled with fresh ricotta cheese. Latte and desserts are on the house. Well, on me. I just can't resist beautiful tooshies."

Java Joe is brimming with baloney. Sapphire stands and catches him totally off-guard with her command.

"Join me in the back room," says Sapphire without any concern about sexual purity.

Sapphire walks toward the restroom area without looking back. With raised eyebrows, I marvel at Joe's perplexity. Sapphire turns and gestures to Joe to come hither, then she places her finger in her mouth and begins sucking. He rushes like a puppy beckoned by its master.

I take one small bite of *cannoli* and Sapphire is already returning.

"What's wrong. Did you flush him down the toilet?"

"Dumbass. He never gave me a chance. He came before I had a chance to unzip him and hold it."

I burst out in laughter, almost choking on my dessert.

Chapter 10

Amsterdam, Netherlands

"Wait until our saucy girl party tonight in the red-light district. You'll piss your undies in excitement," says Sapphire squeezing my hand.

"Amsterdam must be the Venice of the north. So many canals. I'm so glad we came."

I love the feeling of my hair blowing in the breeze. Perched on the canal cruise boat I smile at all the happy people walking or cycling along the banks. Everybody looks so energetic. Every ornate building is distinctive under the blue-sky dreamscape. Young people are sitting on the canal bank, their feet dangling in the cool water.

"This is my third time here," says Sapphire, "I love the people, especially the women. They are quite liberal here, not like America where most women are prudes who sit on their sofas texting gossip and complaints to each other with only a mutt to keep them company."

Indeed, the locals appear relaxed and social. Many are feasting in the open bistròs, immersed in conversation enlivened with bottles of beer.

"Emily, look at that," says Sapphire pointing her finger toward the shoreline.

My eyes capture the spectacle of neon lights that automatically switch on at dusk. I feel like I'm in the center of a bright, spinning galaxy. I extend my arms outward wanting to touch the celestial attraction.

"Easy, girl. Don't fly away on me," exaggerates Sapphire.

Amsterdam, with its labyrinthine streets, is wonderfully chaotic. It's a treasure-trove begging for discovery. The diversity, the insane traffic, and the noise adds to the city's charm.

"Here's where we get off. I'm hungry. How about you?" ask Sapphire.

"Famished."

We dine in a back-alley restaurant. The food is good. Not too expensive.

Sapphire looks at me like I'm a lost child, the focus of an Amber Alert.

"Have you ever thought of going back to Italy? My God, your uncle is the Pope."

The statement doesn't resonate with me. It stunned Sapphire when I first told her.

"Sapphire, it's no big deal. I've never met him. I told you. I had wanted to go to Italy in the first place to spite Renzo. Actually, I didn't think he would have even come. I didn't know any of my relatives. Witches, warlords, policemen, priests. Boy, they turned out more screwed-up than any family I know. I guess small villages breed incestuous relationships and behavior. Maybe it's genetic."

"My God, weren't you surprised to learn that Renzo was also your cousin?"

"I sort of fell in love. We tied the knot. We had two beautiful kids and twenty-five years later I find myself related to the man."

"How is it that you're so casual about all of this?"

"Sapphire, we never knew. Besides, our irreconcilable differences were psychological not physical. He always accused me of acting like a teenager. That I only treated him like a bank machine. That I would flirt with other men right in front of him. That I enjoyed creating drama. Really, I just wanted passion, respect. I wanted to feel important."

"I understand but why not suck up to the Pope once you discovered your connection? You'd be famous. Maybe kings, queens and presidents would invite you to their palaces."

I shrug my shoulders and suck on my lower lip.

"Do you know that my mom, suspecting my unbalanced trajectory, wanted me to be a nun when I was young? Did I ever tell you that? She even sent away for literature and application forms."

"No kidding. I'm glad that never happened. Tell me, do you ever think of hooking up with Renzo again? The guy obviously loved you. You know, you're quite a challenge to live with," states Sapphire.

I'm more annoyed than amused.

"You're starting to sound like my mother. What's the saying? 'You can't go home again.' I only need something or someone to numb past pain. I have you for that. At any rate, I doubt he loves me anymore."

"I do love you. Maybe, the two of us can convince him? Men love threesomes," says Sapphire sincerely.

Renzo strict sense of morality floods my thoughts.

"Renzo's mind doesn't work that way. He hates buffets."

I chuckle as Sapphire rises from her chair.

"Emily, let's walk along *Warmoesstraat*--the street never sleeps."

Outside, the view is mind-blowing. How else can you describe the outdoor urinals? It's reported that more than a dozen deaths occur annually from ignoring the urinals and peeing in the canals and drunkenly falling in. For dessert, we smoke legal, Dutch weed while walking toward party central in the red-light district—the most touristy, pick-pocketed quarter of Amsterdam.

Within moments I hear tourists verbalize their hormones, addictions, and preferences:

> "Disgusting.   Why don't they shut
> down this place?"
> "Best money I ever spent."
> "It's their choice."
> "I'm going fuck me one."

I lock arms with Sapphire. I'm chilled by the airstream that funnels down the narrow streets. I need an anchor of sanity amidst the craziness.

The atmosphere is uncensored. Raw. Men, young and old, window shop to select women. Beautiful brothel women being considered like loafers in a shoe store window. It's legal prostitution. There's color coding to the extracurricular madness. Red lighted windows display women. Purple lit windows advertise transgender pickings. Red and purple together means everything is negotiable.

We slip into one sex palace for our anticipated girlie show. Beer buds, boobs and AGWA cocoa leaf liqueur is everywhere. The sounds and smells are loud, intoxicating. I watch several ladies stumble their way to the dance floor. Some women wear penis caps, most wear provocative or skimpy clothing but all of them are smoking weed. Several screens display projected peep shows. Boy and girl. Girl and girl. Boy and boy. Orgies.

Every female is whooping and howling, shaking booty, hugging, groping, kissing, dancing under the waterfall in a wet T-shirt contest, flashing boobs.

The DJ ramps up the music with heart-pumping basslines as the live sex show begins on stage. A dozen sexy male strippers with taught muscles and tight buttocks, wearing nothing more than colored condoms, prance under the spotlights. Startling sound and gyrations of wall and ceiling spotlights electrify the joint. In unison, the crowd screeches 'Do it!' repeatedly.

Sapphire yells in my ear in competition with the racket.

"Vegas has its porn conventions but this is the girl party center of the Universe. Enjoy! Let loose. Go over the edge. We fly back to New York in two days."

After the first number, the dancers jump off the stage and start mixing with the crowd. Girls grab at penises. Fellatio heaven. Several raise their skintight skirts above their waists and push their G-strings aside and began thrusting their pelvises. Many of the dancers capitulate eagerly.

One girl pops her head around Sapphire's shoulder, and looks me straight in the eyes.

"Would you like to have sex with me? Right here? In the bathroom if you prefer."

I burst into a smile, lunge at Sapphire and give her my most sensuous kiss.

Chapter 11

Trump Hotel, New York City

I feel lonely. My lost dreams are all I have. I feel as if life has screwed me.

"Emily, are you ready? I'd like us to be early for these gentlemen. They're powerful businessmen and drop-dead gorgeous hunks."

It's as if my reflection in the mirror is an illusion. A facsimile of me.

"Almost. Just a little bit more blush."

Sapphire is jubilant. She anticipates her special guy. I think she might orgasm before he even arrives.

"Remember, some clients are loony bins so if I reach for my left earring that's the signal to meet me in the restroom. And if I say 'dance with me' it means we need to get out of there really quickly. I can vouch for my guy but his friend is a newbie. Same goes for you."

"Gotcha."

Sometimes I feel like I'm on the outside watching a movie of my messed-up life. I remember hanging out with my friends as a teen and being threatened with arrest for smoking weed in a parked car. The cop backed off when he could not find any concrete evidence aside from the reeking smell. In those days, peer pressure controlled me. Girlfriends easily irritated me because they wanted juicy stories to tell to other friends. I realize now that they really didn't care about me.

I remember one particular girlfriend, Domenica, who conspired with me. She was older than me and would sign me out of school acting as my sister. We'd dash away in her car and just hang out. She would always ask if anything interesting was happening with me. I felt the need to impress her, to perform. She would incite me to be prankish, sometimes even videotaping my wild behavior. She even encouraged me to run away as soon as I turned eighteen. I didn't. Domenica ended up pregnant, fat and fatalistic. I escaped her fate because of my late puberty.

"You're totally beautiful. You don't need any more make-up."

Sapphire peeks into the bathroom but she's eying my tits and ass, not my face.

"I'm not you, Sapphire. Whites do crack and I need all the help I can get."

"If I didn't know any better I'd say you're

racist. Come on, hurry up. I hear your date passes out Benjamins as tips. I want some of those denominations for ourselves."

The two-bedroom Manhattan suite with floor-to-ceiling windows, thanks to the largesse of our gentlemen in waiting, overlooks Central Park. Everything about the room is spacious, spectacular, and sumptuous. I would never want to settle and rest here. This is performance central not home sweet home.

"Okay Sapphire. I'm ready. Let's go."

"Finally. I was thinking of masturbating if you dallied one moment longer."

"I'm not surprised."

The gents are waiting for us in the hotel's signature restaurant. Moody ambient lighting reflects from the ceiling-mounted fixtures radiating a comfortable mix of brightness and shadows that gives the totally white décor a depth of character.

One of the men who has dreamy green eyes targets Sapphire and stands to introduce himself while his companion remains seated and detached. His razor-sharp cheekbones remind me of a hawk. He has a chocolate-brown tan, an acute stare, wears gaudy accessories, and an offhand appearance. The younger handsome man with the great smile and stubble addresses Sapphire and then me.

"Sapphire, please sit here. My name is Tony and this is Roberto. What's your name young lady?" he gestures toward me.

"Emily," I say softly.

Roberto, continuing to remain seated, feeds on my nervousness.

"Aren't you a porn star?" he lusts.

The question confuses and unsettles me. My legs twitch beneath my red Bodycon skirt with a side slit. Sapphire giggles but, thankfully, changes the topic.

I remain disoriented throughout aperitifs and dinner. I cannot rid myself of the feeling and image of being carrion to this bird of prey whose eyes gawk squarely at my boobs. I have had enough. I begin fiddling my earring. Sapphire picks up on the cue.

"Emily, I need to freshen up. Join me."

I feel myself breathing again. I nod.

In the ladies' room, I unravel. I light a joint and inhale deeply.

"You're kidding, right? That guy looks like a Rottweiler. He gives me the heebie-jeebies. Not someone you'd like to go home to. You seem to know who he is. Do you?"

Sapphire skirts the question.

"Get a Cockapoo if you want to be happy when you come home. You haven't given him a chance. Loosen up. I think Roberto is rather mysterious. He certainly is confident. He'll open up once we're upstairs. I bet his steely look extends to other body parts. You might really enjoy the ups and downs of a stiff ride."

Chapter 12

Trump Hotel, New York City

Part chameleon and part manipulator, Roberto's disposition edges on impulsive and rude. He is without charm or sophistication. Emily's concern is growing into raw fear.

Sapphire and Tony abscond to one of the bedrooms within minutes of returning to the suite. Soon, the sex is loud, even sensual if you credit the rhythm of the moans. Sapphire's exaggerated sounds are for Tony's ego. His resonating bass drum noises escalates in concert with her audible, cymbal-like exclamations.

Roberto pours a glass of champagne. He drops two white pills that bubble in the sparkling wine before approaching Emily as she looks at

Central Park below and the night sky through the ten-foot tall window. He presents her the glass.

Emily, jumpy, catches her breath as she watches Roberto walk away and settle on the sofa.

"Have you and Tony been friends a long time?" she asks trying to be casual.

Emily wants to be sociable, and also drown out the noises from the other room. Roberto doesn't respond.

"Are you married?" Emily digs deeper.

Roberto just stares.

"I'm divorced. I had a husband who believes in the concept that it's cheating even when there's no actual sex. He believes that socializing with someone ultimately leads to attraction and that it's betrayal right from the start. He's hung up on reputation and trust. His ideology drives me crazy to this day. He would consider me being here just for a drink a form of adultery. What do you think?"

"Do you want another drink?"

Emily glances down at her empty glass.

"I didn't realize that I'd finished. I suddenly feel relaxed. Actually, I feel good. I feel like dancing."

"I want you to stop talking and take off your clothes," commands Roberto.

Emily is shocked. She opens her eyes wide. She clenches her teeth. Chills and nausea befall her. She feels her heart pounding at an alarming rate. Her visions blurs. Emily loses consciousness and collapses onto the floor like a rag doll.

Roberto stands and walks over casually. Mimicking caveman courtship, he grasps Emily's limp arm and drags her to the second bedroom.

Chapter 13

Metropolitan Hospital, New York City

Valeria, wearied and old, sits in the hospital family waiting room, knitting a skull cap of red, blue, yellow and white yarn hoping to bring life back to Emily after her near-death experience. She recites a short prayer for her daughter with each stitch anxious to return to Emily's bedside once the doctor completes his daily assessment.

"Hello Valeria. How are you?"

Valeria's jaw drops open. She looks at the old man in his signature wardrobe: black dress sneakers, low rise navy blue trousers and a cream-colored polyester windbreaker with an embroidered stylized 'E' on his lapel. She bursts into tears.

"Emilio, my God! What are you doing here?"

Valeria cannot contain herself. Her crying becomes hysterical. She drops her knitting to the floor. Emilio rushes to sit next to her. He drapes his arm around her trying his best to console her. But nothing works. The tears blur her vision.

"I came to New York on business. I called Toronto hoping to visit before returning to Italy. Your employee, Emma, told me you rushed here because Emily was seriously injured. She said Emily is in a coma?"

Valeria simply nods.

Emilio releases his own bad news.

"Giuseppe and Esterina have been killed in a car accident."

Valeria's shock is profound. She is so traumatized that she stops crying.

"I had to go to Toronto on behalf of Mamma Teresa and handle all the post-death arrangements. No one has told Renzo yet. They want me to deliver the news when I get back," says Emilio.

Before another exchange, the doctor enters. He is slim and humorless with white pale skin that matches the cold pallor of the visitor's room. He hesitates. Valeria recognizes the reticence.

"He is family, Doctor. Please, what news do you have?" asks Valeria.

"Taking ecstasy, particularly this crude version, can be very dangerous. It is not unusual to see muscle breakdown, kidney, liver or heart damage. Sometimes after ingesting MDMA patients can suffer from brain damage or even death."

The doctor pauses for dramatic effect.

"The good news is that we have stopped

the internal hemorrhaging and prevented any cardiovascular collapse. The tearing from the sexual assault is considerable but there are no signs of HIV infection. Regardless, she will need months of rest and recovery. We have no way of determining her emotional and psychological health before she wakes up. I surmise that she will regain consciousness once the buildup of toxins has been flushed out of her system, perhaps in two weeks."

The doctor makes an uncharacteristic statement.

"I believe prayer will help."

Emilio notices a yellow gold crucifix ring on the doctor left hand as he turns to leave.

Turning to Valeria, Emilio asks for assistance.

"Valeria, I read the police report. No charges were laid. It made no mention of a sexual encounter. It did, however, mention another woman, Sapphire Mandeville. Valeria, do you know who she is? Where she lives?"

"Her and Emily are business partners. They share an apartment somewhere in Greenwich Village. She called me to tell me about Emily. I don't know more than that."

"Do you have any of her personal belongings? Her purse?"

Valeria responds eagerly. She's glad to be with someone she knows.

"Yes. In the room. In the storage locker. Why?"

"Good, there may be an address. I would like to talk to this woman. I just want to make sure she's okay."

Emilio offers an empathetic smile which quickly fades as he hugs Valeria in consolation. His look of suspicion is unmistakable.

Ozzie Logozzo

PART FIVE

"Holy water cannot help you now." – *Florence + the Machine*

Chapter 14

Greenwich Village, New York City

The area is filled with enough middle-market fashion retailers to make shopaholics swoon. Designer boutiques, unique restaurants and funky cafes are all within walking distance. For Emilio, waiting outside for the shops to close and shoppers to disperse could bring unwelcomed attention. However, sitting and waiting patiently inside Sapphire's apartment is integral to his planned ambush.

Looking out the kitchen window, Emilio waits in the dark drinking a beer he found in the ruby red refrigerator. The pricey accommodations are fully-equipped and overly furnished. There is a clash of cultures and a really strange taste for design. The eccentricities in color and chattels defy all rule books and make Emilio shake his head. Depending on the room, heavy textile Persian carpets with ornate geometric designs lend support to ultramodern sofas and circular chairs in a mishmash of colours—cherry red, orange, and avocado green. Contemporary decorative glassware rests on antique tables encircled with chrome chairs. The rooms appear to sprout floor vases in ceramic, glass and metal.

Emilio sneers at the garish décor. He is not impressed and is quite content to keep the lights off.

It's 2:45 a.m.—approaching last call—and Sapphire is not home yet. It doesn't matter. Stamina is one of Emilio's stellar qualities. Doctors have always kept Emilio waiting. It's understandable that a high-class call girl should show the same disrespect.

Finally, he spots a yellow cab stop half a block down the street. Emilio recognizes her. Her appearance matches the photos around her apartment, particularly the large framed selfie taken in the red-light district of Amsterdam. With her purse draped over her shoulder, she carries a Gucci gift bag in one hand and holds down her short skirt with the other. Regardless, the wind causes an upskirt, Marilyn Monroe moment with her flowy, black mini dress. Emilio tilts his head to the side as he smirks slightly.

"*Ciao bella*," he nods and whispers.

Emilio watches her climb the half-dozen steps to the building's front door. Once inside, he hears her place the bag on the floor. She belches as she enters the kitchen, her hand trailing along the wall in search of the light switch.

Emilio, standing in the dark on the opposite side of the door frame, punches out her lights before her fingers find the light switch. He takes one last swig of beer and then carries her to the suede sofa. Her nose looks broken. Her cheek is swelling. Some blood trickles down her nostrils.

Emilio returns to the kitchen, rummages about and finds a pasta pot. He is pleased. He fills it with cold water and returns to the living room. He sits on the coffee table made out of old wood pallets. Placing the pot on the floor, he methodically removes his gun from its holster and attaches the silencer. Emilio sighs. He places his weapon on the coffee table. Then, he picks up the pot of water and dumps it on the Sapphire's face. He quickly covers her mouth as she regains consciousness.

"I just want to talk, Ms. Mandeville. Nothing more. I want some information, that's all. If you attempt to scream, I'll blow your brains out. If you cooperate, I'll let you live. Understand? Nod, if you understand."

Sapphire is terrified. She sees the revolver. She agrees.

"I know you and Emily were together. I know she was drugged and raped. I know you signed the police report. I know there was no indictment. There is not even mention of the Johns."

Sapphire looks offended.

"Johns? We're not prostitutes! We are escorts. We provide companionship. There's no sex unless we want it. We are professional and one hundred percent discreet. Who the hell are you? What do you want?"

Sapphire recoils against the backside of the couch as Emilio picks up his gun. His frown deepens into a scowl.

"You talk a lot but you're not saying anything. I don't like women who talk a lot."

Emilio presses the gun into Sapphire's lower abdomen.

"What are their names?"

"Mister, these guys are mobsters. I didn't know before but it became obvious after Emily's ordeal. They control the cops. They're ruthless."

Emilio lowers the weapon's barrel between the woman's thighs.

"Do I look like a harmless, old man to you?"

Petrified, Sapphire shivers.

"It is really simple. Their names or a bullet in your snatch. Pick."

Chapter 15

Little Italy, New York

Emilio frustrated from an eerie, sleepless night rises in a sweat and sits at the edge of the bed. The reel in his mind loops footage of Emily's limp figure in the ICU using a breathing apparatus and her mother crying, tears dripping unto her needlework. He growls revenge for his wayward niece. He will hunt the jackal and castrate him. But, business first.

The Mulberry Street hotel is a short walk to the center of Little Italy. The small hotel's exterior is non-descript. The location suits his purpose. He is expected to lunch at the *Diplomatico* restaurant, a favorite of the New York crime bosses.

Just before noon, Emilio strolls outside on a scouting expedition. He is torn between his mission and his vendetta. The initial fear of facing the American Mafia leaders is displaced by his inescapable need for self-healing through retribution. He talks to himself like other homeless souls wandering the streets.

"I will hurt you. You think you're safe but I will find you. I will cut your puppet strings, *Pinocchio*. I don't care which *Geppetto* might be your protector."

A sign on the *Diplomatico* door reads, *Closed Today for Private Function*. Unperturbed, Emilio, sees bodies inside along with a bartender, taps on the glass pane. One of the men mouths an obscenity while pointing to the sign. Emilio, steadfast, knocks again.

The man, livid, opens the door and confronts Emilio.

"Can't you fucking read?" shouts the man.

Emilio holds his ground.

"Is that any way to speak to your guest of honor?" says Emilio.

"What? Who the fuck is you?" the man challenges.

An older man with gray hair intercedes and slaps his cohort at the back of the head.

"Show respect."

He squares up to Emilio.

"Forgive my ill-mannered son. Kids today dress like bums and have no regard for their elders or traditions. I recognize you from the photo sent by the Vatican. You're early. We were expecting you in an hour. Please come in, Mr. Orsetti. Let's have an *aperitivo* at the bar while we wait."

Emilio sees several waiters passing through black, heavy soundproofing curtains, setting up a rectangular table of more than a dozen place settings. At the bar, he opts for a *Campari* on crushed ice. The old gentleman, giving an understanding wink to the bartender, is served a *Cynar* cocktail.

The *ristorante* has a busy decor. Though homey, the place is cluttered. Knickknacks, images of statues, pictures, and paintings combine in a charming, casual, hoarding atmosphere.

"Mr. Orsetti. Formalities. You understand."

The old man is standing with arms spread-out.

Emilio stands and faces the old man raising his elbows to the side. The old man pats down Emilio's body with open palms, including underarms and crotch and crunches loose clothing to ensure there are no hidden objects.

Afterward, they engage in small talk about Italian food and drink and the lost art of homemade winemaking. The old man never says his name and Emilio doesn't ask. They are interrupted. The meeting is ready to begin.

Emilio is escorted through the curtains into a private dining room. All chairs are occupied except for two closest to the curtained entry. The patriarch of the assembly, seated at the opposite end in front of a mantled fireplace, stands and walks over. He shakes hands and kisses Emilio on both cheeks. Emilio sees a backdoor entrance handle through drawn curtains that fully encircle the windows and walls.

Back on his throne, the patriarch introduces

the entourage, one by one. Emilio's disregards the names except two, which trigger physical and psychological inner turmoil.

"Tony Fiscella and to his right is Roberto Falco."

Tony, through tinted eyeglasses, is operating a computer with various attached gadgets encased in an aluminum briefcase. Emilio recognizes it as an anti-eavesdropping device. Roberto sits stone-faced, legs spread as if getting oral sex from a female under the table.

"My name is Santo Rofalo. I am *'capo consigliere'* to the five families. All these gentlemen are *capi* in charge of various territories, interests, and enterprises. We, the advisory committee, will hear what you have to say and then make our recommendation to the Commission. You may begin at your leisure."

Emilio sits upright, both hands on the table's edge with fingers interlaced. He starts to speak.

"I am only a messenger for an aggrieved Pope who asks for your assistance and support in stopping the violence against the Italian people and the Sicilian Mafia's determination to overtake the Papacy and control the Vatican bank. We are experiencing crime-plagued cities, turf wars, corruption, bribery, and killings on an unprecedented scale. In order to prevent open warfare and tremendous suffering, the Pope is offering a straightforward solution of mutual benefit."

Emilio pauses. He reaches into the inside pocket of his jacket and withdraws a piece of paper, opens it and begins to recite.

"His Holiness requests the following:

- *Discontinuance of direct links and support to the Italian Mafia*
- *Redirection of all means of trafficking and distribution to channels outside of Italy*
- *A levy of ten percent on all Vatican Bank deposits for the construction and maintenance of hospitals, schools and other social services*

In appreciation for collaboration on all these points, the Holy See is prepared to ensure the following:

- *No sermons or reprisals from the pulpits of any Catholic Church*
- *No publication of the records and secret archives of the clergy*
- *No suspension of Vatican City diplomatic passports*
- *No cessation to international deposits to the Vatican Bank*
- *No freezing of accounts in Italy or Germany amounting to billions of Euros*
- *No forensic analysis of assets nor publications of asset holders*
- *No interruption in Vatican investments in America or sell-off of its stock holdings*

The Pontiff, in God's name, reserves the following rights:

- *Freedom to deal with its own criminal cardinals and bishops*
- *Freedom to recover stolen 'Peter's Pence'*

> *cash and securities placed in Berlin banks*
> - *Freedom, in association with the carabinieri, to deal with the Italian Mafia as God commands*

These are the terms I have been asked to present to you. Along with them, I have correspondence, sealed and signed by the Pope, expressing his blessing to the people of Little Italy. This should be taken as a guarantee of the accuracy and integrity of my message. Thank you for listening."

The crowd is stunned into silence. Roberto, the personification of the *malocchio*, (the evil eye) breaks the peace.

"My *nonna* warned me about the horns of the devil, *le corna*, when I was young. She said, 'never trust the number 13. It's Satan's sign. The proposal has thirteen points."

Emilio remains composed. His eyes scan the gathering, momentarily pausing as he locks eyes with each *capo*.

"I count thirteen men seated at this table. In my world, *Stregheria*, the number thirteen is associated with nature and the goddess of fertility. We believe it brings luck and prosperity."

Roberto is not consoled.

"So, you admit to being a witch?" asks Roberto.

Emilio is offended but responds with feigned politeness.

"Last time I looked I had balls," replies Emilio.

Santo interrupts before passions inflame and negotiations break down.

"Roberto, enough. Emilio, your message has been received. Let's break for lunch. You will have an answer tomorrow at sunrise."

The other *capi* begin to relax.

"How will I get it?"

"Consider it a yes if you are still alive," says the consigliere.

Chapter 16

Little Italy, New York

Emilio offers the cabbie $200 more than the meter rate.

"I'll give you another two hundred dollars at the end of the ride."

The taxi driver is spooked.

"Look man, if some shit is about to go down, I can't. I got a wife and kids."

"Nothing like that. I'm a lawyer working on a case. My client's husband is cheating on her. I need to follow him to his destination to serve him with court papers. Okay?"

"What do you want me to do?" asks the cabbie.

"Exit Mulberry, left on Canal and left on

Baxter. Park immediately as you enter Baxter, just before the laneway on your left. It's the only auto entrance on the block and it's a one-way street. We will be able to see him exit in front of us and then I want you to follow him. Nothing more than that."

The cabbie consents.

"I'll have to charge you for wait time as well."

"Agreed. Let's go."

It past an hour before the car brigade begins its exit through the backstreet. Emilio, having removed his sweat-soaked suit jacket and restraining tie, perks up.

The afternoon rising temperature combined with the stomach-churning, heat exposure in the auto thankfully ends before sickness sets in.

"Here they come. Get ready," states Emilio.

The cabbie stops working on his crossword puzzle and turns the ignition key. The motor doesn't crank. Emilio is upset.

"You're kidding me?" says Emilio.

"No, no. It's okay mister. I'll turn the engine," reassures the driver.

The cabbie unlocks the hood, gets out and lifts the hood. Incredibly, he removes one shoe and starts smacking the battery terminals. He runs back inside, left shoe in hand, throwing it on the passenger seat. Again, he starts the engine. The starter kicks in.

"See? No problem. Just needed to shake off the corrosion around the terminals."

Emilio is relieved and a bit impressed. He slinks lower in the back seat.

"Okay, heads up," says Emilio.

Lincolns, Cadillacs and Mercedes line the cavalcade. There's one hyper car, a Bugatti.

"That's the guy, in the blue, black sports car. Follow it," commands Emilio.

The cabbie is alarmed.

"Mr. Falco? Mister you're playing with dynamite. I can't. You're going to get us killed."

"You know him?"

"Everybody knows him. He has a reputation. He owns the *Inferno* nightclub on 58th Street."

Emilio hands over two hundred dollars before leaving the cab. The driver is dumbfounded.

"That's all I need. I can handle the rest."

Chapter 17

Inferno Night Club, New York City

It seems that there are almost as many bouncers as there are patrons. Bachelorettes clad in their best designer looks and men on the prowl flirt, drink and dance to the vibe of eardrum splitting music. Wall and ceiling lasers discharge captivating, undulating spider light beams onto the walls, ceiling and dance floor like phantoms sweeping for souls.

Roberto, standing at the foot of a stairway, marvels at his prized possession. With the over crowdedness, the hefty cover charge and the overpriced drinks, business is booming.

Two oversized bars, on the ground floor and another on the horseshoe-shaped open loft are jam-packed with people queuing for watered down cocktails. Hooter-type girls with uplifted bras serve bar and raise profits.

Roberto is dressed in a black business suit, black shirt and no tie. His cell phone rings. He cups one ear, attempting to cancel the background commotion.

"Hello."

Roberto smiles.

"I'll be there in an hour."

He calls over one of his supervisors, whispers a short message and leaves without ceremony. He is headed for the neighbouring parking lot, two buildings down, shielded from street view by an aluminium paneled fence. It begins to drizzle. He hastens his pace.

With his hand on the car door handle, Roberto drops to the ground from a mighty knockout punch to the temple.

The outdoor lot is secluded and guarded by two video cameras that have already been disabled. There are no pedestrians on the High Line, elevated park path at the back of the lot.

Perched over the limp body, the stranger gags Roberto with a dirty rag then slides a black hood over his head. He unbolts Roberto's pants and pulls them down to his knees. With repeated sawing, the stranger amputates Roberto's penis. Blood covers Roberto's genitals. His head and body bob in excruciating agony. His muffled screams are futile.

The stranger, penis in gloved hand, unlocks the gate and walks out onto 26th Street. He drops the penis into the street gutter. As he walks from under the overpass the night light flickers on Emilio's satisfied face.

Ozzie Logozzo

PART SIX

"There is no guidance in your kingdom." – Thievery Corporation

Ozzie Logozzo

Chapter 18

Vatican City, Rome, central Italy
'In the beginning'

"Werner, it's for the best. It's our only option to save your standing. It's a sacrifice for Sister Lidia, I know. It's painful and humiliating but she can now serve God in ways she couldn't undertake as a nun. We can't give infidels license to besmirch the Church."

Werner looks at Pope John Paul, his dearest of friends, as if aching from excruciating bodily and mental pain. He feels helpless and paralyzed.

"John, I have failed you. I am so sorry. Please forgive me."

Werner, crying in his hands, beseeches death.

"Father, into Your hands I commit My Spirit."

"Werner, you are not Jesus. You are a

righteous man, a Cardinal, who has fallen into temporal sin. I cannot forgive your evil but I know that God has forgiven you. God is merciful. We deserve punishment but He doesn't punish us. Indeed, He blesses us. His mercy is rooted in His love for us. His mercy triumphs over all judgments."

The two men are sitting side by side in the Pontiff's private chapel. Both sprout white hair in need of a trim. Werner wears a plain black cassock with buttons and scarlet piping. His skull cap, saucer shaped, *zucchetto*, rests crushed on his lap. John Paul's white vestments are in sharp contrast. His white *zucchetto* is complimented by a matching *pellegrina* (short shoulder cape) adorned by a large, silver oxidized pectoral cross of Christ the Good Shepherd carrying the lost sheep on His shoulders. Through stylish bifocals, John Paul leafs through the Bible.

The private chapel located down the hall from the Sistine Chapel is the Pontiff's ideal, iconic sanctuary for reflection and prayer. It is an artistic wonder with religious frescoes crafted by masters such as Michelangelo. Werner is captivated by the image of St. Peter who is secured to a cross about to be raised and crucified upside down, so as not to imitate his God, Jesus Christ.

"Werner, 'Peter's Pence' contributions amount to millions of dollars annually. The largest donations come from the United States. The specific amounts are logged at our end," says Pope John Paul.

The Pontiff pauses to choose his words wisely.

"I am very old but not blind or oblivious. The

silence in our ministry shrouds financial corruption. There are heavy losses in our bank. Well, I don't need to detail the obvious to you. You are head of the Vatican bank. Nor do I place any blame on your shoulders. Regardless, one day, a Pope, younger and stronger than I, will investigate and tackle the misdeeds. For now, I propose you do for yourself, Lidia and your unborn child, what my enclave of Cardinals have been doing for themselves for years."

Werner's pattern of gasping and holding his breath softens.

"Sister Lidia wants to name the child Paola if it's a girl and Paolo if it's a boy, after Saint Paolo who was blinded but had his sight restored."

"Very apropos. We too shall turn misery into majesty."

John, after rising, places his hand on Werner's shoulder.

"My friend, as head of our Vatican bank, you have the means to harbor your woman and child with material wealth beyond their imagination," affirms the Pontiff.

After a moment of silence, the Pope adds a lasting thought.

"Pope Leo X was candid when he said, 'It has *served us well, this myth of Christ'*. Let's not squander our continuing good fortune. You must stay with me. After all, you or your designate will become the next Pope."

The Pontiff rises and slowly saunters out of the chamber. Werner is left in wonderment.

Chapter 19

Monastery at Lake Como, Bellagio, northern Italy

"When I left New York, I felt good. Relieved, to be alive. Today, Paolo, your words have killed me."

"Emilio, for crying out loud, look at what you have done. You made a flawed deal with the Americans. We need ruthless retaliation not tender, tiptoeing diplomacy. You should have come to me before blindly following Renzo's instructions. Hiding out in this villa has proven ill-advised."

Paolo reflects on the turn of events and his falling fame.

"The Mafia is our real enemy here and abroad. Don't be fooled by media accounts of its demise. Renzo is a tenderfoot. He does not know what he is doing. The suspension of their activities is illusory. Only a fool would believe the Sicilians have scattered or abandoned their activities and mission.

Whatever trauma you inflict on them, it is fruitless if it is not severe and sustained. Like salamanders, they are masterful at regenerating lost limbs. These human lizards are immune to injuries. They must be destroyed beyond redemption," preaches Paolo.

The Abbey grounds are tranquil. There are no bystanders. Paolo and Emilio are walking down an isolated path far away from the monastic complex. The herbal medicinal scents of citrus arbours, flowering azaleas and rhododendrons are lost in the breeze. Paolo momentarily suspends his diatribe as they tunnel along the dirt path lined with cypress trees.

"I'll straighten out Renzo," says Paolo speaking to himself.

Seconds later he turns to Emilio.

"I want you to set up a meeting of the *Stregheria* council at Gandolfo. Do you think you can do that?" Tell them I'm alive. We are going to go to war with the Mafia."

Emilio's silence deepens with each shaming statement.

"Rather than a settlement, I will give don Filippo a rope to hang himself."

After excruciating moments of stillness, Emilio speaks.

"Renzo has been quite engaging and passionate. He is admired as a champion. His plan has gained everyone's support. He is not rash or hasty. Rather, he's bold."

Paolo perceives the not so veiled criticism of his past leadership.

"Don't lecture me on his governance qualities. Get that meeting convened and I'll derail my wayward bastard."

Chapter 20

Trento, Italy
'In the beginning'

I don't understand why I'm here. I was slapped at the back of my head by that old bag of a nun librarian while coming down the staircase during the mock fire drill. My friends played in the schoolyard while I was pulled aside and brought to the principal's office. Oh, the embarrassment! I bet everyone in the courtyard is talking about how the principal of our school, *istituto Davido Santo*, is going to make an example out of me. For what? I didn't do anything!

The principal's office is rather small. Next to the window, there are two black, filing cabinets, side by side and taller than me. There's a large crucifix on the side wall. Jesus' hands are pierced and bloody.

Did the Romans really do that? Why tie someone on a cross when you could more easily spear them to death on the ground? Were Romans trying to shame Jesus? I can't believe God let the Romans do that to His Son. It doesn't make sense. Maybe the Bible is wrong?

I've been waiting for over an hour sitting in front of the principal's plain wood desk. I like his rotating stool. I wish I had one.

It's already afternoon recess. Why are they making me wait? My bum and back hurt from sitting on this stiff chair and my legs are falling asleep. I'm hungry too. Although we are on the second floor, I wonder if the other kids can see inside the window. Are they too busy playing soccer?

Loud voices entering from behind me make me jumpy.

"I'm sorry I startled you, Paolo. Sister Carmela tells me you broke the rules during the fire drill."

The principal is a portly priest. His swollen nose makes him the perfect example of too much drinking. Still, I always liked him, especially after showing us how to kick a soccer ball with power. Except for his white collar, his wardrobe is all black, even the rosary around his neck. He does wear his belt ridiculously high. I guess he's trying to cover up the excess fat around his waist. He should play soccer with us more often.

As for Sister Carmela, I can't look at her. I'm afraid her *malocchio* (evil eye) will cast a terrible spell on me.

"So, Paolo, do you know what you did?" asks

the principal.

"No, Father."

"You spoke during the fire drill. The rule is clear: there is to be no talking during the fire drill."

I'm still don't understand the rule. What if you need help?

"I only asked my friend what exit we were using," I explain.

"Rules only work if they are not broken. You've left me no choice but to give you the strap."

Is he kidding? He must be kidding? I didn't do anything wrong! I was simply trying to follow the fire drill procedures.

From his top desk drawer, the principal removes a tanned and tattered leather strap. Shit, he's not kidding.

"Stand up, Paolo, and hold out your right hand. Palm up."

I must be nuts. I obey. After several lashes that sting like hell, he misses and hits the inside of my wrist. Still, I don't cry. I am surprised to see that Sister Carmela asks Father to stop. I feel ashamed.

"You can go back to class now," says the principal. He sounds sorry.

I turn to leave the office and instead of going back to class, I walk directly to the front double doors of the school. I leave. I have made up my mind never to return. My mother will understand.

During my dreadful walk home, I begin to cry. My hand is bruised and swollen. What lesson have they taught me? How is this Catholic? Fuck God. Where was He? He didn't help me...just like He didn't help His own son.

As I approach the apartment building where I live, I notice a priest sitting outside on the steps. There is also a *carabinieri* squad car parked in front and two men in suits hanging around. What now? Have they come to arrest me for truancy? There are groups of people scattered and talking and whispering to each other while staring at me.

The priest sees me and offers a gentle smile. He walks over to me. The *carabinieri* stand their ground.

"Hi Paolo."

How does he know my name?

"My name is Father Werner Marin. This morning after you went to school, your mother had an unfortunate accident. The coroner has taken her away. She called me in desperation. I came as soon as I could but I was too late. She has passed away."

The priest hugs me. I hear his words but I can't cry any more. I have no tears left. Why is he hugging me?

"There is a place, a monastery in Germany, where you will live. You won't be going to school any more. Professors from the University of Trento will come and tutor you. There you will receive excellent care and the best education that money can provide. It's the least that I can do," says the priest. His last words were said so softly I could hardly hear him.

No more school? I like that idea! But why?

I notice flashes of light are coming from one of the windows in my house. Then I see him. A photographer is walking around snapping photos. Beside him is another man in a suit, with a writing pad. What is he sketching? Both of them are wearing white gloves.

No more school? Maybe God did listen to me. That's great!

This priest has the same last as me. What a coincidence.

I begin to understand why the onlookers are whispering.

I hear the whispers.

'She was seen walking in deep depression.'
'She cried often.'
'She often talked to herself.'
'She mumbled suicide.'
'She hurt herself.'

My mamma is dead but I have no more tears left.

Chapter 21

Monastery at Lake Como, Bellagio, northern Italy

"Deciding to make a deal with the Devil is desperate but the killings must stop. We need a diplomatic approach. We need a ceasefire before we end up in a civil war," says Renzo firmly.

Paolo doesn't answer. Emilio is his mouthpiece.

"Renzo, you can't coddle criminals. The Mafia is hell-bent on doing its own thing. They commit crimes for their own cause. They're greedy and want power over all of us. They're ruthless", counters Emilio.

"Emilio, apt description. How different is that from us? It's a shared, progressive cancer. Like locusts we have swarmed the land and infested our ideology. We have hurt family and friends. We have killed women and children and men of the cloth. Crime and punishment, splendid sermons and stately speeches are futile. Mafia groups such as Cosa Nostra and the *'Ndrangheta* continue to flourish in spite of bullet-riddled bodies," replies Renzo.

Renzo is addressing the troubled Emilio but is really speaking to his father who remains silent.

"Perhaps you should let your father take over. After all you need time to grieve for the loss of your parents in America," urges Emilio.

"It's too late for me to help my adopted parents. I will help ensure my step-sister receives the best quality of life that money can buy," pledges Renzo.

Renzo now turns to face Paolo.

"As for my biological father, he is dead wrong. Ruling by force is doomed for failure. It's delusional to wield a big stick. In all instances, speaking softly and showing respect is more effective," affirms Renzo.

There is span of uncomfortable silence.

Renzo feels the need to fill the void.

"Emilio, the Mafia flourishes because of our sorrowful social and economic state. If you want the culture of *La Stregheria* to reign in its place, we can't continue like this. It's madness. We must forge new relationships. Unpleasant? Yes, but it is better to correct the situation than to make it worse," says Renzo ending his sermon.

Paolo, stands staring out the shed door. He turns and finally speaks.

"You are naïve and incompetent. All those years of schooling, training and preparation in America has made you soft, not the worthy leader I was anticipating. You live in your imagination. I base my actions on reality. I'm anchored to the factual not the probable. Your head is lost in drama. I deal with specifics."

"I agree that details are relevant but their significance must be assessed in light of our future design. Facts are never simple. They change with changing circumstances and decisions must be strategic not impulsive," argues Renzo.

Emilio, moping but still attentive, isolates himself from the debate. He sits on a pile of planks in front of agricultural apparatuses: sickles, grubbing axes, barrels, hand cultivators, digging forks, hoes, rakes, shovels, trowels, pruning scissors, hammers, spikes, and a plant box. The previous emptiness of the tool shed in the monastery courtyard is now the scene of a courtroom challenge between father and son.

"Our strategy is clear: Disenfranchise the Church. Disperse its wealth. Destroy Catholicism. Return to the family values of *Stregheria*," demands Paolo.

"No argument there but actions need to be weighed and calculated for consequences and impact. We cannot afford ambiguity," says Renzo calmly.

Paolo erupts into a fit of laughter.

"Oh, my God. Who is the professor here? You clothe your naiveté with picturesque words. Is my son prepping for a Ph.D. tutorial?"

"Did I just hear you plead to God, father?"

Paolo, foremost the professor, lectures his beliefs.

"In all my years, I have never underestimated the enemy. Reformers and revolutionaries, far wiser than me, have shared great advice on not undervaluing an enemy and overrating one's abilities. The guiding principle is Machiavellian; crush them before the opportunity escapes you. If you think the Mafia families—now disorganized— are not going to regroup and retaliate then I wasted my money on your military studies. You should have paid more attention to your professors. You are one man running on imagination—a confused perception of reality—not reality, past or present. The nail is useless without the hammer."

"Paolo, we differ in understanding and perception of the same situation. You think you know what is best but you don't. We cannot afford an endless escalation of battle. This is not a personal affront. Your strategy is slanted and slippery," says Renzo with increased frustration.

"Listen here, Renzo. I am not going to let your criticism distract me. I want to be clear; personal affront does not enter into it. I have no need to reassert my philosophy and I will make sure that detractors like you do not take me off course," affirms Paolo.

"You are content in your complacency and self-sufficiency. You do not allow yourself to be called into question by anyone. I will not lead others to walk on your philosophical quicksand," insists Renzo.

"Enough is enough. No one knows reality better than me. You are an ungrateful son. I saw to it that you received military training and a military lifestyle. I entrusted Giuseppe to provide you with an unconventional education. You were trained in Martial Arts. You served in the armed air reserves and learned to fly and to parachute. You mastered war studies and military history. All for what? To become a pacifist? I should have discounted you when you dropped out of the Military Academy to study social sciences. Or were you kicked out for constantly rebelling and fighting? Whatever. I have zero tolerance for you. It's my fault for impregnating the wrong slut," declares Paolo.

Renzo, unable to contain his festering emotions, snaps. He lunges at his father and lands a nose-breaking punch to the face. Like a jack rabbit, Emilio jumps on Renzo with a rear-choking grip yelling 'Stop it'. With ease, Renzo tucks his chin, spins, bends his knees, and flips Emilio to the ground. He stands like a majestic book between two fallen bookends. He speaks first to Emilio.

"I never asked for this job. I accepted it half-thinking. I may have failed in my marriage but I have never failed in my worklife. Use one of your operatives and get a message to don Filippo. I want a face-to-face meeting. Get it done," instructs Renzo.

Looking at his fallen father, Renzo threatens.

"You staged your own death. Now remain dead and out of my way or I'll kill you myself."

Chapter 22

Berlin
'In the beginning'

It is an old warehouse with a high ceiling strung with plenty of brewery memorabilia. The venue hosts a ball for gays, lesbians, bisexuals, prostitutes, sodomites and perverts. The scene inside is willfully wicked. The drinks are abundant. The smog from the smoking and soot from the grandiose fireplace corrode the nostrils and lungs.

Paolo, large stein in hand, is vibrant and nearly sloshed. He pounds the beer mug on the wooden table to accentuate a point while his laughing compatriots, equally festive and rowdy, add to the bar's pandemonium. Even the waitresses, wearing full face paint and burlesque costumes, listen in and add irreverent annotations.

"The abuses and indulgences of the Catholic Church demand not just reform but eradication. Protestantism is not the solution. *Stregheria* is the answer," rambles Paolo.

Two bottled blonds, curvy waitresses chime in while placing two large pitchers of beer on the table splashing suds on the tabletop.

"Paolo, you're drunk again," says one waitress.

"You're barking the same song. Stop driving us crazy. Save it for your university classes," says the other waitress.

Paolo is unshaven and morose. He is detached, self-centered. He's growing angry that his intelligence is being undermined.

"I am not a buffoon or a punk. Listen up. We are all damaged by Catholicism. We are a cliché. A joke filled with guilt and shame. Everlasting sinners. Go ahead, laugh in my face but the facts are indisputable. Religion has emotionally and psychologically abused all of us," insists Paolo.

Pointing at the waitresses, he shouts.

"You two are fornicators for losing your virginity outside of marriage!"

The more bodacious server retorts after planting a kiss on Paolo's cheek and flashing her boobs in his face.

"But I like sex," she says brashly.

"Precisely," says Paolo. "You are a whore because you are not a virgin, a Madonna. But behold! Sex isn't sacred. It's natural. All religions are dogmatic and narrow-minded. The simple truth is that only nature is positive and non-judgmental."

One male crony, craving comfort and status quo, challenges.

"So, you'd have us believe in witches and the evil eye and have us wear charms or necklaces of onions?" says the young man.

"It would certainly improve your smell," expands Paolo.

The male companion is offended. He drowns his pain with another beer.

A female friend, like an exaggerated method actor, mimics her words with an elaborate performance of a frenzied sorceress.

"We would curse and cast spells, incant rites and call upon powers of light and darkness to destroy evil and bring good fortune," she says unable to control her own merriment.

Flailing her hands about with a crazed look of Satanic possession she spins off into an incantation.

"A pinch of pollen, a pinch of sand, scrapings of lavender blossoms steeped in rosemary and rue, bring us blessings—wait, I forgot a pinch of periwinkle—here under the full moon, cleanse my soul and grant me pleasure."

She grabs her crotch.

"Maybe a man with a really big cock," she says with finality.

The burst of laugher and loud applause is dashed as Paolo dumps his drink on her head. Paolo is sucker punched by the male companion. Several beer showers are launched like a wave from table to table until the bar is plunged in a total pandemonium.

While servers attempt to separate brawling patrons, an overly-aggressive and beefy bouncer hammerlocks Paolo, who is punching and kicking, and drags him to the side entrance, tossing him onto the pavement. The bouncer notices a cut and blood on his arm. Consumed by anger, he takes revenge by unleashing a volley of game ending kicks. Spent, he re-enters the club and slams the door shut.

Paolo is rolling back and forth on the ground in a fetal position, shockingly laughing.

"If you can't handle me now, imagine when I'm at my worst!" he shouts skyward.

PART SEVEN

"Don't get too close. It's dark inside. It's where my demons hide." – Imagine Dragons

Chapter 23

Lido di Tarquinia beach, Tarquinia

Domenico, smelling the fresh seaside air stands in pajama boxers on the large canopied terrace overlooking the Tyrrhenian coast, the sea of the Etruscans. He turns, heart still throbbing, and gapes at his companion's backside. She is standing naked admiring a tall bowl of chrysanthemums on a vintage French bistro table. Her curvy, nubile body glows.

"Did you send yourself these flowers or do they belong to your wife?" asks Regina from inside the apartment.

"I'm not married. *Crisantemi* represent sorrow. They are for my father's grave. He died a long time ago. I'm going to deliver them later."

Recalling her father's funeral, bereavement teardrops drip down her face.

"I'm sorry. Mine was killed not too long ago. But, let's not be sad especially after last night," says Regina.

Regina turns to face Domenico who is standing and smiling just outside the balcony door.

"It was wonderful. You initiated feelings I never experienced before," blushes Regina.

Domenico, over-eager, re-enters the room. Regina jumps him and wraps her arms and legs around him. The bond doesn't progress much further.

"Oops, I think I'm leaking again."

Regina jumps down and hurries to the ensuite. She leaves the door open.

"It okay. Just a bit of leftovers."

Domenico raises his voice.

"Regina, you know you're very special, don't you?"

"What do you mean?"

Domenico is leaning against the bathroom door frame while Regina remains seated on the toilet. He enjoys her hanging tits.

"Well, you wear dark and sinister clothes. You portray yourself as glum, yet, in private, you are fun and flirty. Naked, everything about you is smart and sexy. It's as if you have two personalities. Perhaps that's why you didn't tell me you were a virgin."

"I do not have a mental disorder."

"No, no. Don't misunderstand. Had I known, I would have made your first time much more memorable and pleasurable. I would have gone slower."

"Believe me, you turned me on. It was quick enough to avoid too much pain. Now go turn on the coffee machine. I want a *caffè latte* with a *crostata*, if you have any."

"Yes, mamma."

"What? Am I your mamma? Do you make love to your mamma, Mr. Oedipus?"

"Don't even joke about it."

Domenico fumbles in the kitchenette. The aroma of espresso preludes the mist of hot milk. He substitutes brownie *biscotti for crostata* and adds a cup of honey yogurt *gelato* with roasted strawberry sauce. As he delivers the tray of goodies to the small terrace table, Regina appears dressed in purple panties and Domenico's sleeveless nightshirt.
She sits on the chair with her legs in a figure-four lock and imitates a therapist by asking a leading question.

"So, tell me about your obsession with your mother."

"I think my step-brother Renzo is the one with the mother fixation. That's why he couldn't hold on to his wife."

"Renzo has a thing for my sister. It's pretty intense."

"That won't last. He's egocentric and demanding. He talks a good talk but he is coldblooded. He tries to show mamma that she should love him more than me and Adamo. Besides his head is elsewhere. He's committed to *Stregheria*."

"I thought that was all antiquity? Stuff for

archaeologists and historians."

"Hell no. My mamma is a Strega and Renzo is the *Stregheria's* commander-in-chief."

Domenico enjoys telling tales out of school. He relishes the surprised look on Regina's face.

"Did he give the order to blow up *Gioiosa Marina*?

"What? How did you know about that?" ask Domenico in genuine surprise.

"Are you kidding? It was all over the news. Besides, the gossip is that the *carabinieri* are in cahoots with *La Stregheria*."

"So, you are not some love-struck, hot, young woman captivated by my charm? In fact, I remember! You totally ignored me the first time you and your sister came to *Piazza Cavour*. In fact, you gave no impression of my existence."

Domenico points his wagging finger at Regina.

"I know who you are," smirks Domenico.

Regina blanches.

"You are some kind of countercultural reporter working for some press syndicate. You don't want my love. You want a news story. Headlines printed in ornate Gothic font. I am your anonymous source of information."

"You regret being my 'Deep Throat', sexual boy toy?"

Domenico chuckles.

"So, for the Italian Gothic Press and my monstrous readers, what news do you have about *Stregheria*?" asks Regina.

Domenico, places his finger to his lips and

leans forward.

"Shh, it's a secret. A secret society of witches and warlords wanting to use the Pope and his crew of priests as puppets for the benefit of society. Renzo is the new leader of the pack. A charioteer lashing out at the forces of darkness."

Domenico leans forward to deliver the punchline *sottovoce* (in a quiet voice).

"They practice witchcraft," reveals Domenico.

With a slight shake of his head, Domenico rests back in his chair. His derisive description changes into soulfulness.

"Sometimes I think the only ungodly benefit they care about is themselves and that I am the only authentic member in this circle of rogues, mamma included," says Domenico.

"If Renzo is new, who was the previous leader?"

"Ah, a question directly from your journalistic playbook."

Domenico hesitates. He shoulders a worried face and halts the banter. His demeanor changes to utmost seriousness.

"Look, Regina. This is serious shit. Absurd, really. You don't want to know and you don't want to get involved. Let's forget all of it."

Domenico is adamant. Regina hides her look of dissatisfaction with a slight smile.

Chapter 24

Trento University, Trento
'In the beginning'

"*Dio mio*, he's the cutest I have ever seen."

"Relax Teresa. Your libido is fizzing over."

Teresa and Maria are rhapsodizing on the sad state of affairs of their immature, male classmates. Seated at the end of an aisle five rows from the front in the small lecture hall, Teresa and Maria spy on every sophomore milling about before the start of the lesson.

"Maria, let's move over one seat and keep the end one empty for him."

The ladies do a quick side shuffle but are quickly disappointed to see the object of their attention rest his portfolio on an empty seat in the front row. Their fascination galvanizes their sexual senses. Maria pinches Teresa who whispers words of delight.

"There is something about this guy...I like him...he's sexy and...he excites me. It's settled. Maria, you can have your pick of the lot but that young man is mine. I'm going to kiss him, and more, before the week is over."

Maria is suddenly unsettled.

"Look, Teresa. What is he doing? He's going behind the lectern. He's asking for trouble."

"Good morning everyone. My name is Professor Paolo Marin, and I welcome you to your introductory class on *Art and Architecture Through the Ages*."

Several co-eds giggle while their male friends roll their eyes. Teresa and Maria look at each other, open-mouthed and wide-eyed. Professor Marin is jovial. He speaks with clarity and expressive hands held high and open, passionately pontificating.

"Our studies will take us to major centers such as Berlin, Vienna and Rome and, although we will examine innovative approaches to art and architecture during the Middle Ages, our focus will be on the Renaissance. We will go in depth on such themes as how the Rococo style spoke to the self-indulgence of the aristocracy and we will end our studies by tracing the trajectory of art and architecture after the Enlightenment. It is my contention that a true understanding of the images we will examine require more than a mere understanding and appreciation of religion and nature. The inclusion and role of sexuality and erotica in art and architecture is paramount. What you may now consider taboo was once celebrated. We will attempt to answer the question: To what extent does desire shape art?"

"Maria, he excites me. He's my aphrodisiac. I'm going to be helpless in his embrace."

A plain plump girl, seated in front, turns around to gossip. Her conspiratorial whisper is soft and uncoded.

"I've heard that our playboy professor is a sexual predator. He has murky ideas on religion and a trail of affairs, some with other professors' wives and daughters. He's a lecher with too much money and attitude."

Teresa leans forward to stare into the gossiper's eyes.

"No man is self-sufficient or secure. Maybe what he needs is an emotionally mature woman. Me! So, get your nose out of my business!" says Teresa.

The gossiper curls away and shivers grateful that the lecture ends as quickly as it started.

"There is no purpose in pursuing our first topic until you have had the opportunity to do some background reading. On my desk, here I have a stack of papers listing resources I want you to look at along with your first assignment due in sixty days. Please help yourself. See you next week."

Classmates scurry to the front to pick up the reference material.

"Maria, pick one up for me. I'm going in to bait my hook."

Maria laughs and scampers to join the bottleneck of students.

Teresa waits until all others have distanced

themselves from *professor* Paolo. Then she moves in and instantly touches his arm.

"*Professore*, you do realize that you are wrong, don't you?" says Teresa.

Professor Marin smiles at the assertive intruder.

"I have been wrong many times before. How am I wrong this time?"

"Desire does shape art but, for the true artist, art should shape desire."

"That's an interesting hypothesis. What's your name young lady?"

"Teresa. Perhaps, we should debate our differing views on art and sexuality,"

"Are you free for coffee tonight?" says Teresa in all earnest.

The professor is awe-struck by the young lady.

"No, I'm not," says Paolo.

Teresa shows no signs of deflation. She smiles with a slight tilt of her head.

"Are you free tomorrow night Miss Teresa?"

"Yes, I am, *Professore*," says Teresa with a wide grin.

Chapter 25

National Museum, palazzo Vitelleschi, Tarquinia

Away from prying onlookers who are charmed by the varied golden geographical panorama of the placid town and its surroundings, *Tarquinian* chapter members of *Stregheria* wait in earnest. Mamma Teresa, the Society's founder, has called an emergency meeting. The museum is closed on Mondays. Assuredly, no outsider will disturb the gathering.

Everyone is scattered. The museum curator, Isabella, sits behind the counter in the gift shop leafing through an oversized volume of paintings of antiquity. The Mayor, Sebastiano, marvels at the sculpture of the Winged Horses. Adamo and Domenico stand and play *Briscola* atop of an

Etruscan sarcophagus that has been acquired from the *Tarquinian* tombs. In the open courtyard, Anna-Maria, *consigliere* and treasurer, daydreams with her eyes closed and head tilted toward the summer sun. Mamma Teresa is approaching, having sacrificed her usual midday nap.

With her attendant remaining on guard outside the museum door, mamma enters the courtyard. The large door closes with an echoing boom. Old age has hit mamma Teresa hard. A pacemaker controls her heart's rhythmic breathing. Her muscles cramp and swell easily. She suffers from arthritis in her left shoulder, left hand and fingers. Publicly, mamma is regal. As a widow, she refused to wear black even on the day of her husband's funeral. She continues to dress her petit frame with color and elegance and has perfectly coifed silver hair. Her appearance speaks of classic, timeless grace—a manner weathered through a great deal of loss and change in her life.

Mamma stops by the ornamental, dry well in the courtyard under the partly cloudy sky to peer in as if expecting to see her reflection. The others swarm to her side like honeybees returning to their queen. She looks worried. They sense the tense mood, frown and wait. No pleasantries are exchanged. They wait for mamma to speak.

"Paolo is alive," says mamma not showing emotion.

There are expressions of doubt and momentary flashes of incredulity. Some perhaps even question mamma's senility.

"It seems that the Mafia was not the only

one in hibernation. Paolo and Emilio faked the *Professore's* death to surprise the Mafia with an unprecedented offensive."

Mamma sits in the chair offered by Anna-Maria.

"This changes nothing. Renzo is still in charge. *Stregheria* will not be driven by one man's contempt for the Church and his single-minded obsession to avenge his mother's excommunication and death. We must rise above Paolo's conflict with the Church."

Sebastiano steps forward with a furrowed brow, shaking his head from side to side.

"Am I the only one confused here? Mother? Excommunication?"

Mamma Teresa speaks *sottovoce* (softly).

"Paolo and I share, as we all do, a common belief that the Church has amassed a huge fortune. It thrives on greed and power. Historically, there have been epic abuses at the hands of men of God. Commandments have been broken. People have been deceived, persecuted, condemned," says mamma Teresa collecting her thoughts before continuing.

"What Paolo and I could not agree on was the specter of a defrocked nun—an image that haunts him hourly. I sympathized but he let his childhood memory control him. He lets his personal vendetta cloud his vision. Rather than move forward and use the Church's treasury for the common wealth, he nurtures his pain. Paolo aims to crush the Church. All because a former nun, his mother, suffered at the hands of the Vatican. She was maligned, ridiculed, and physically abused by her 'Sisters'. Battered and emotionally mutilated, she almost lost her baby. The father, a Cardinal, remained protected. His mother hung herself when Paolo was a teenager. It is said she could no longer face herself after countless acts of humiliation.

Paolo's father, serving as the financial director of the Vatican bank, was protected by the Vatican. No one berated or shamed him. Tremendous wealth was set aside for Paolo's upbringing and future. There was enough wealth to serve an army of heretics. Paolo's guilt and hatred of clerical celibacy distanced him from his father. They rarely met. However, Paolo was able through his father's influence to secure positions in the enclave for his two friends and priests, Pio and Virgilio. I think you can surmise the rest."

The museum curator speaks what is on everyone's mind.

"Do you think, with their mole, Luigi, out of the way, that the Mafia will try to kill Renzo again?" says the curator genuinely wondering what the future might bring.

Mamma, certain of the inevitability, answers with a look of resignation.

"No doubt. They will try to kill me as well. That's what Adamo thinks. That's why I now walk with a bodyguard. After all, it's easier to kill us than to control us," says mamma Teresa.

For reasons of his own, Domenico walks away from the group. He is visibly upset.

Chapter 26

Tarquinia, Italy

Anna-Maria trembles. Her cell phone, perched precariously on the edge of the coffee table, is vibrating. It's Domenico. Domenico's previous text forecast the reason for this call. She can't avoid him any longer.

"Hello," answers Anna-Maria.

Without ceremony, Domenico launches his tirade.

"I don't understand. I have been trying to reach out to you and the family. You know it would make me happy to have Regina at our meetings. It's one extra person. It's not a big deal! Why are you prejudiced against me and Regina?"

"Domenico, if Adamo asked for his girlfriend,

Emma, to attend our meetings I would be equally hesitant. We discuss confidential information. Emma and Regina are outsiders. They are not family yet."

"You think I keep secrets from Regina?"

"Domenico, please understand. It's premature. You have known Regina for such a short time. As *consigliere*, it's my role to give sound advice. The family has always accommodated you more than you have ever reciprocated. You are a high demanding individual. You sometimes ignore polite, respectful behavior. Your request will cause an imposition. Surely, you must see that?"

"What are you talking about? I contribute! Regina should not be your concern. You should trust me."

"Domenico, your relationship with Regina is your concern as is Adamo's relationship with Emma. Emma and Adamo have been together a long time yet Adamo has the good sense not to ask mamma, through me, to participate in our organization."

"I don't give a damn about Adamo and his slut. You're a guardian of *Stregheria* which is all about giving but you are not opening your arms to me and my girlfriend."

"Domenico, you're asking me to do more for a stranger than you are prepared to give to the family. You cannot expect me to advise mamma on such an ill-conceived idea. Philanthropy does not equate with inappropriateness. You want this woman to attend private meetings where highly sensitive information is tabled. Domenico, think critically. Be reasonable. Don't be such a puppy. You are choosing this woman over the family."

"Oh, okay, that's fine. You'll have plenty of room at the meetings for others. I'm no longer coming. You and mamma can enjoy yourselves."

"Domenico, how much did you tell this woman about us?"

Anna-Maria hears some muffled dialogue just before the line goes dead. A chilling sensation creeps in. She mutters.

"Domenico, what have you done?"

Chapter 27

Tarquinia, Italy
'In the beginning'

It's my choice to be emotionally exhausted and desolate. I could have stayed in Trento at the University to continue my affair with my professor— star-crossed lovers Teresa and Paolo. It all began innocently. We shared a common interest in art and history. He was mature. I was infatuated. It felt right to dine with him. It felt right to travel with him. It felt right to sleep with him.

What was at first appealing to me, soon became repulsive. I began to see what I interpreted as his initial charisma to actually be conceitedness. Other women desired him and he accepted their flirtatious advances. I don't think he deliberately sought their company but he certainly did not refuse them. I tired of the games people played. It made me physically sick. I felt let down. It broke my heart.

We started arguing. What was once cute became hurtful. Perhaps, men are genetically incapable of being monogamous. Do they crave perpetual stimuli to battle against emotional atrophy? If so, I can't accept it. Am I mentally disturbed? He did accuse me of having heightened sensitivities and illogical thinking. He called me eccentric. I did react with dramatic changes to my mood. I became crude and critical. Sometimes we had the best make-up sex ever but more often we drew farther apart. When I missed my period, I left town.

Now I work at my sewing machine making dresses for the sugar mamas of *Tarquinia*. In my spare time, I pour over books about classical antiquity, particularly ones about religion and witchcraft. I do think I'm a *Strega*. Paolo preached about *Stregheria*. Its philosophical beliefs became a passion of mine.

I alter and mend a garment hoping to finish before sunset. My ground level apartment is small and comfortable. Everything is within steps of where I sit at my sewing machine under the sole window.

I'm awakened from my sewing trance by three loud knocks at the door.

"For crying out loud, your dress is not ready yet!" I mouth to myself.

Rich bitches think I can be disturbed anytime.

I harness my anger and answer the door oozing politeness. But, I stand in shock. He's got me losing my balance.

"Hello, Teresa."

Paolo is rugged and hot. He is incredibly irresistible. His killer smile is not calming. It was once when it was reserved for me but I have seen the same smirk given wantonly to other women.

"Paolo, what are you doing here?"

"May I come in?"

Why? Does he expect some fairy tale ending? We fought bitterly. I severed the torment. Why is he here? I step aside nodding my head, weak in the knees.

The room is scantily furnished. There is no place to sit aside from the solitary chair beside my sewing machine. We lock eyes. No doubt, he is uneasy with my coldhearted reception.

"You left the university without a word. It took me a while to find you. Thanks to my friend, Emilio, in the *carabinieri*, I tracked you down. Well, I want you to come back. I need you. I love you."

I remain speechless.

"Say something."

Paolo steps toward me but I retract like a wounded animal.

"You lied and manipulated me. You don't care about me. You were never serious about me. You just don't like being rejected," I yell.

"I still don't understand. I didn't do anything wrong. I never cheated on you."

"Yes, you did. You can't connect with just one woman. You lent your attention to all other women, especially the pretty, young ones. I will not be spurned. I will not stomach that kind of emotional immaturity. Yes, it's characteristic of a lot of men but it's not the type of man that I can love."

"Are you saying you don't love me?"

With a straightforward gaze, I shatter any last hope Paolo harbors.

"Paolo, I believe in your cause. *La Stegheria* is morally right and fair. Catholicism is spiritless and oppressive. I will remain a dissident and help build the movement here in *Tarquinia* but your flirting friendships with other women goes beyond my limitations. Be honest with yourself; you like those sorts of affairs. I don't! It's dishonest, dishonorable and disloyal. Our relationship isn't just troubled. It's broken. No, no, no. I don't love you anymore. We can support *Stregheria* by phone. We don't need to see each other. Please leave. Now."

Paolo, jolted, turns toward the door. He stalls. He puts one hand in his pocket but quickly withdraws it empty handed. He releases a surrendering sigh and departs without further talk. I watch him walk away. From the window, I see him pull and open a small black jewelry box out of his pocket. Its contents shine but not bright enough to alter his behavior.

I shut the curtain and sob. Why did I lie to him? I do love him. Why can't I be a normal person like everyone else and accept people for who they are? Am I crazy?

I walk toward the full-length mirror adjacent to my sewing machine. I begin to unbutton my loose-fitting, knee length, dress shirt. Tears are dripping down my face, neck, and chest. They come to rest on my obvious baby bump.

I stare at my reflection. Is this what shame looks like?

Chapter 28

Stazione dei Carabinieri, Tarquinia

Adamo is sitting at his large oak desk tending to a phone call as I walk in. I interrupt him and speak openly.

"Adamo, I'm doing nothing wrong. I have a right to a private life with whomever I choose."

Adamo cups the phone receiver, gives me a stern look and tells the caller to call back later as I continue my outburst.

"Have you told mamma about your Emma? Would mamma approve of you dating a China woman? No. I doubt your runaway sweetheart is as sweet, warm and innocent as she portrays. That Asian flower of yours probably has more dark roots than my Regina. So, what if Regina is a Lupo. You can't punish her for the sins of her father."

"Domenico, I'm speaking to you as a brother, not a *carabiniere*, so please try to understand. Regina is an UNSUB; an unknown subject. As uncomfortable as it might be for you, these matters take time. You know your Regina for what she is now, but not for what she may become."

"You're talking nonsense!" blurts Domenico.

The phone rings again. I wait as Adamo scribbles notes on a pad. The desk plate with his name and title is as pretentious as the other gaudy knickknacks strewn about his credenza and bookshelf. Why does he need two computers on his desk? What's with that oversized tricolor flag? A simple desk pennant would suffice. That huge pewter and wood enamel plaque on the back wall with the Italian boot and *carabinieri* crest is intimidating enough, as are all those decorations and medals on his jacket hanging beside the large monthly planner whiteboard. Military echoes of authority and power invade the space and my mind. This need to repress me, enrages me. I am no less important to the family for simply being an owner of a bar and restaurant.

I have had enough. I don't deserve this cold and distant treatment. I stand and leave.

"Domenico, wait. We need to talk."

Without turning around, I raise my hand over my shoulder and give my brother the finger.

Chapter 29

Civitavecchia, Italy
'In the beginning'

Paolo, having bought a ticket at the *Tabacchi* cigar store, boards the bus just outside downtown *Tarquinia*. The bus is bound for *Civitavecchia*. He greets the driver Giuseppe, Teresa's neighbor, with a question.

"Is the final stop near Forte *Michaelangelo* in *Civitavecchia*?"

Paolo, knapsack slung over one shoulder, sits to the right of the driver.

"This is the right shuttle. The fortress is quite a structure. Commissioned by the same pope who commissioned Michelangelo to create the frescoes in the Sistine Chapel ceiling. Are you an art enthusiast?"

"I am but my interest today is the ancient city's beachside promenade. I'm told you can buy some of the best breakfast in nearby cafes. I hope to share one with someone I don't quite know yet."

"Ah, *l'amore*. A blind date?" asks Giuseppe of the stranger.

"Sort of, but not quite. I want to propose an incredible offer of lifelong security and wealth."

"My goodness. Sounds like some lucky woman is going to be overjoyed today," says Giuseppe with piqued interest.

"Actually, it's not a woman. It's you, Giuseppe," says Paolo.

Giuseppe is dumbfounded. He looks in the rear-view mirror at the passenger who sits smiling. Further talk is interrupted as the bus comes to the next stop. Two dozen school children with their teachers and volunteers board on their way to a day-trip.

While Paolo focuses his attention on the beautiful countryside, Giuseppe drives anxiously, overwhelmed by suspicion.

Upon arrival at the *Civitavecchia* port transfer point all the passengers except for Paolo scurry to disembark.

"This is the last stop. From here, I'm reassigning to another route at the town depot," says Giuseppe.

Paolo reacts with a pleasant smile.

"I know. I'll get off there with you."

Seeing Giuseppe's troubled indecision, Paolo elucidates.

"Giuseppe, what's the worst that can

happen? There's nothing to worry about. You are in full control. You're not certain of what's coming but don't let that uncertainty distress you. I assure you that my offer is a generous gift. A blessed benefaction that is difficult to refuse."

At the final stop, Giuseppe, somewhat shaken, confronts his stalker with conviction.

"Look, I don't know who you are. I'm just a poor bus driver. I have no money."

Paolo interrupts Giuseppe who is openly frightened.

"Giuseppe, relax. I'm Teresa's friend. Renzo's father."

Giuseppe is awestruck. His goofy, shocked expression makes Paolo chuckle.

"Please, lend an ear to me and I will tell you a story. It ends happily for Teresa and brings your family riches you could only imagine."

The men stare at each other. Finally, Paolo breaks the silence.

"It's only a short walk to the promenade. I know a café that serves the Italian breakfast of champions. *Zabaglione*. Marsala wine with egg yolks. That and a side of mixed berries followed by an *espresso* will uplift and inspire us," says Paolo smacking his lips.

"I only have thirty minutes before my next shift."

"I only need fifteen but I'm betting that after our talk, you'll want to retire and seek other opportunities."

Giuseppe is dazed. His confused expression persists.

Paolo boldly wraps his arm around Giuseppe's and steers him to an outdoor café within walking distance of *Forte Michelangelo*. Seated outside at *Ristorante da Vitale* off *Via Aurelia*, Giuseppe is all ears. The early morning sun overheats his right side that is not fully covered under the restaurant canopy. Paolo sits, remains serene, and places his knapsack on the empty chair between them. He recites his incredible story of falling in love with one of his students. Paolo offers detailed recollections of amorous adventures, lovers' spats, dreams and aspirations, of his pre-empted attempt to propose followed by Emilio's investigation with the doctors and the certainty that Renzo is his son.

"*Dio Mio*," is all that Giuseppe could muster.

"Strange, we talked about one day having a family. We always said that if it was a boy we would name him Osvaldo. I thought she would even though she didn't want me around."

Giuseppe comes to life.

"Oh, Paolo, she did intend to call him Osvaldo right up until the month before he was born. Then that crazy mid-wife—I think she was a gypsy—convinced her otherwise. She said that if her baby was a boy and she didn't name him Renzo, a noble name, then he would be stillborn. Teresa was frightened. She is very superstitious. She believes in fate but not religion. She just didn't want to chance it.

No matter."

"We picked Osvaldo because it's a noble name. Osvaldo is a ruler and lover, not a player. A trustworthy person who only wants to make his woman feel special," reminisces Paolo.

Paolo pauses to sort out his thoughts.

"Listen Giuseppe, she never told me she was having my child. She's such a stubborn woman. You have witnessed the fact that she cannot handle him on her own and she doesn't want to be with me. I know you love the boy. Your kindness and care is recorded in all the hospital records. You've treated him as your son. Your sister in Canada is sponsoring you. Take my son with you before she kills him. It's best for everyone. I beg you."

Paolo's eyes fill with tears but he quickly regains his composure.

"Tell me, Giuseppe, what do you think of my offer? There are two million *lire* in the knapsack for you to take home today. There will be two million *lire* deposited in your account every five years for life. Teresa will work for me, for my *Stregheria* movement, and earn prosperity and gain the prestige that she desires more than the love of family. All I ask is that you adopt Renzo and take him to America. There you will provide for his upbringing and education, monies that I will send separate from the wealth I promise you and your family. We will be in regular contact through emissaries. I will only specify the nature of the education required of him. All else I entrust in you."

"Paolo, how am I going to convince Teresa to give up Renzo?"

"I have already arranged for it. With the help of *Carabinieri*, the local priest, Renzo's school teacher, and others, Teresa will draw her own conclusion. I need your support and that of your wife to make this work."

"Mamma mia," Giuseppe's eyes are closed, "What a surprise. This is going to take Esterina's breath away."

Chapter 30

Tarquinia, Italy

I can feel myself stiffening with rage. This matriarch dresses and presents herself in celebration of life. She should be dead. She, along with her philanderer and her bastard son will be dead. They are responsible for the death of my father and mother.

"Please Regina, have a seat. I asked Sebastiano, our honorable mayor, to bring you here because I wanted to talk to you privately without Domenico and one of his testosterone tantrums," explains mamma Teresa while Sebastiano shuffles off to the side.

Bitch! Murderer! Mamma Teresa is pointing at one of the two empty chairs in front of the mayor's Baroque desk. Its luxuriously decorated with gilded gold. The worktop is spotless. There is nothing more than a solitary lamp on one end that isn't even plugged in. No papers, no calendar, no phone, nothing. I doubt the mayor is a master of organization and productivity. I'm guessing that city problems must play second fiddle to matters regarding *Stregheria*.

I slip into one of the grandiose burgundy background chairs. I can feel the lush comfort of the hand-upholstered front and back. Mamma Teresa sits in the other. We are separated by a small table. It, too, is very detailed and ornamented. Indeed, the entire office looks palatial. I fit into this regal display chamber of power and control as much as a pauper in a palace.

The mayor offers me a drink.

"May I get you a drink? Water? Coffee?" says Sebastiano.

This pretender wants to serve me. Well, I'm as much deserving as any other visitor. This mesomorph needs to consume less sugar with his cups of coffee. I notice a contemporary coffee machine housed within the open four-door antique oak bookcase behind his desk that is flanked by the Italian flag on a pedestal.

"A cappuccino," I say emphatically.

"In the afternoon, *signorina*?" asks Sebastiano.

Is he acting like an executive or is he just being arrogant? What's so suspect about my response? Northerners abide by ridiculous rules, especially when it comes to food. I'm certain he would ridicule me if I asked for a shot of *Sambuca* in my coffee after a plate of spaghetti and meat balls.

"Yes," I repeat myself.

He submits but his head shake from side to side is unmistakable. Perhaps a swift kick to his butt would add to his tremor and dislocate his brains. Another thought redirects my focus. This over-controlling woman is powerful enough to have the mayor run her errands.

My Domenico feels inadequate and emotionally empty because of his mamma Teresa. I feel sorry for him that her opinion of him is more important than his own. What a wimp. But, his anger and self-induced depression are proving useful to me.

Mamma Teresa takes back control of the conversation.

"I was watching you enter the building from the window. You came in only seconds before Domenico entered the *Carabinieri* station across the street, no doubt to speak to his brother," says mamma Teresa.

So? Does she expect me to comment on brotherly love? Perhaps I should tell her how Domenico feels sidetracked by her ambitions. How he feels ignored and rejected by a social cause he doesn't have the patience or desire to understand. How he desires to feel the comfort of family and friends, screw politics and power. Mostly, how he rejects Renzo's fortuitous rise to power.

The cappuccino is served. I take it without thanks. Mamma Teresa continues her discourse.

"After years of suffering the community's

moral outrage, I have earned social acceptance. My peers see me as a hard-working, proud person who only wants what's best for everyone. You are new to our family circle. Understandably, you and I lack trust. With Domenico, you have a romantic relationship. You trust each other. Other members of our family plead for me to trust you as well. I don't. Call it mother's intuition. I don't trust you or your sister. It's not your fault cara Regina but your family is Corrado. Mafia."

"Was," I say sharply.

"Yes, yes. You may think me insensitive. I prefer authentic. I see things sharply and I voice what I feel. I don't see what others anticipate or expect. I see what is really there."

"And what do you see in me?"

"Excellent, I like directness," says mamma Teresa with a hint of surprise.

Mamma quenches her thirst with a sip of water before continuing her denunciation.

"In you, I see discomfort. I see a depth of energy steaming and searching for an escape valve. I think your angst is consuming you. You want revenge. That's why you're here."

She's a bitch, but a smart one. I'll give her that.

"You love playing with words, don't you?" I ask.

"My dear, young lady. We are mired in crosshairs. Indeed, we are at a crossroads but let me put it simply so there is no play on words, no double meaning, no misunderstanding."

What the fuck is her majesty serving now?

"I want you to forget about Domenico, forget about *Tarquinia*, and forget about seeking revenge. Accept your fate and move on. You wouldn't like the other alternative."

"Which is what?" I demand.

"If you remain, I will conclude that you want to continue with your ill-conceived 'an eye for an eye' grudge. Therefore, you will be accused and arrested for attempting to resurrect your family business by trafficking in narcotics. You will rot in prison until you are so debilitated and depressed that your release will be disappointing. I urge you to go home. Have many *figli* with someone of your kind and forget about us. You have twenty-four hours to decide," says mamma Teresa with dilated pupils, stiff body language and no breathing.

What balls. I'm sure with her *carabiniere* muscle she could follow through on the threat.

The matron stands with a surge of unforeseen strength. She looks down at me.

"Your thoughts are obvious. Yeah, I am a bitch. Now get out of my office," commands mamma Teresa.

Her office? Incredibly, I find myself saying the absurd.

"Thank you."

PART EIGHT

"There will be an answer, let it be." – Paul McCartney

Chapter 31

Spormaggiore, northern Italy
'In the beginning'

"Wow, Fausto's what a banana kick! Emilio, you're useless between the sticks. You didn't even see the soccer ball coming," laughs Pio.

"Shut your mouth if you don't want my boot up your ass. Fausto got lucky. He doesn't even know how he did that," taunts Emilio with a sweet smiling face and an outstretched arm that is chopping up and down. The message is unequivocal: *Ma va' là* (cannot believe it)."

"Listen here little brother. That instep kick was a bomb and you know it. Your problem is you're too short and your balls scrap the turf, slowing you down," Fausto joins in.

"Speaking from experience, are you?" counters Emilio.

Virgilio is bent over suffering from shortness of breath partly from exertion but mostly from laughter. Paolo, who has dominated the play, avoids the banter, removes his jersey, and suggests a break as he walks toward a corner patch of grass that overlooks the road and the cemetery.

The soccer field is between the village church and the cemetery. All three sit on the hilltop overlooking the valley of farms that stretch out far below.

"What do you get when three Christians team up with a carabiniere?" chuckles Paolo then answers his own joke.

"Three tight asses and a short keeper," laughs Paolo.

"What the hell does that even mean? Are you calling me short?" provokes Emilio.

Paolo pretends empathy.

"Relax, little one. I don't want you to blow up a storm," adds Pio.

Virgilio, as is his custom, teases his youngest brother.

"Emilio, you should be endlessly grateful. Escaping from the bedroom window without your pants is like serving the smoking gun on ring bearer pillow. If Paolo had not intervened, that head of yours would have been guillotined and your other head would have been blown off its shoulders. Next time you screw around with another man's wife make certain he's not capable of hunting you down with a loaded shotgun," says Virgilio preaching as if from the pulpit.

"Money can overcome most obstacles; don't

you think?" Paolo muses.

The statement is rhetorical. No one responds. The men settle under the shade of a clump of trees. Emilio removes his soccer cleats. Pio is tempted to crack another joke on Emilio's stature but restrains himself.

They open leather Bota bags of red wine and pass around grilled polenta, pre-cut wedges of aged cheese and lemon pine nut biscotti. Fausto appears preoccupied. He stares at the mountain range but clearly his mind is elsewhere as he munches his food methodically. Virgilio eats much too fast, predictably suffering from heartburn and an expanding waistline.

Everyone is aware of the true thrust of today's scrimmage. After months of deliberation and debate, everyone is expected to declare their commitment to Paolo and *Stregheria*.

Paolo addresses the group.

"You guys know that you're my family. Honestly, I consider myself blessed in knowing you. Sharing my good fortune with you has given my life a purpose and a direction. Pio and Virgilio are guaranteed servants of God within Vatican City, thanks to my father. Pio has been appointed a member of the Supervisory Commission of Cardinals of the Vatican Bank. Perhaps, one day he will be elected president of that directorate and oversee the bank's activities. Virgilio is going to serve inside the Pope's inner circle, along with my father who is the Prefect of the Papal Household and, de facto, overseer of the bank," says Paolo letting his statement sink in before continuing his discourse.

Moments pass before Paolo awakens the group from their reverie.

"Your brother Giancarlo has rejected my offer. He wants to stay in Spor and take care of mamma. Admirable. It's not typical for a man to refuse wealth and power. Tell me Fausto, as the oldest, what will you do?" asks Paolo.

Fausto, as if examining his own unconscious thoughts and feelings, confesses his internal dream.

"Paolo, I am not interested in symbols nor in temporal, political life. I will always be indebted to you for helping my brothers and my mother escape abject poverty. Without you, we would have all starved or lived a dying life. Your generosity has been profound and incalculable. Your hope, your *Stregheria*, of helping others is admirable. It is a just cause. But I am not a political animal," says Fausto pausing for emphasis. "I don't want bureaucracy to shield me from the people I want to help. Men are shaped by their ideas. Yours are clear. I admire you for your conviction. I am still in a state of bewilderment. I don't know if eradicating the Catholic Church and its dominion will uplift everyone's life...or add misery. I don't know what moral and spiritual consequences will ensue. I don't know if it will help or negate Christian love and charity. I do know what it means to be hungry. I understand a mother's tears. I believe that hope is a tool of empowerment."

Fausto looks down at his packed refreshments. He looks up again and speaks remorsefully.

"I want to help the poorest families,

particularly the children and mothers, not just through economic activities but by providing solace. I have committed to the society of Missionaries to Africa. I will help people deal with their hurt and suffering. I can think of no better way to thank you than to help other exploited and vulnerable people," says Fausto.

Paolo smiles but his disappointment is noticeable.

"Paolo, I have no doubt that you will succeed in your undertaking. My evangelical soul rages within me. I must go. Please understand," pleads Fausto.

Emilio's restlessness is stretched to the limit. He intervenes.

"Look you guys are much too religious. God, Devil, Hell, Heaven are all vague spiritual concoctions. The real mystery of life is woman. Take it from me: you guys need to get laid. Except Pio, of course. Pray, how is that student nun of yours?" asks Emilio.

Pio whips a piece of cheese at his brother.

Emilio protests casting a pronounced, bewildered look.

"What? What? Do you want me to arrest you for assaulting a *carabiniere*?"

The men burst into laughter. Only Virgilio remains confounded, less by Emilio's rude remark than by Paolo's plan to transform the Church. He diverts his own misgivings.

"It's time. We men of God must prepare for tomorrow's liturgy, the one and only time we will be afforded the blessing of having three brothers deliver a mass. Praying is much less strenuous on my body. I know Emilio is not inclined but, Paolo, why don't you join us in scripting the sermon?" asks Pio.

"Thanks, but no. Someone has to watch Emilio drown his sorrowful goalkeeper skills in alcohol. You guys go ahead. I'll roll Emilio home after his second pitcher of beer."

Virgilio, Pio and Alfonso head for the church rectory. Paolo and Emilio beeline for the bar in the *piazza*. Pio, guessing Emilio is at a safe distance, whips the soccer ball at his back.

"You suck, Emilio! You need to face the ball and stop trying to block it with your big ass," laughs Pio. The others join the amusement.

"Let it go. I need to talk to you. In private. About my child," says Paolo as he clasps Emilio's forearm.

"What?" says Emilio giving a look of surprise.

"I'll explain inside. I'm thirsty," responds Paolo.

Across the *piazza*, diagonal to the church, Emilio and Paolo enter the *Dolomiti Pizzeria*. Emilio is walking as if intoxicated by Paolo's disclosure. The Black Devils brigade are just exiting. The deafening roar of their single-cylinder, Otto-cycle engine motorized bicycles clashes with the accordion music coming from within. They seat themselves at a table removed from the card playing area. The sign on the wall reads, 'Chi beve birra campa cent' anni' (Those that drink beer live to 100).

A plump server with wild hair wearing a black blouse, a grey pleated skirt and a white waist apron appears promptly. The specialty, any time of the day, is '*pizza della Chiesa*' with a hearty ale to match. Emilio, rattled, is passive and devoid of his characteristic sexual banter with all waitresses. With orders placed and feeling Emilio's apathy, the young woman leaves. She is visibly unhappy.

"Emilio, I went back to *Tarquinia* to see Teresa," begins Paolo.

"You gave her the ring this time?" brightens Emilio.

"No. She had a bigger surprise for me."

The waitress, now with too many blouse buttons undone, returns with beer and glasses. She eyes Emilio but he remains oblivious to her flaunts. Looking up Emilio dismisses her.

"That's all for now," says Emilio.

Emilio turns to Paolo adopting a conspiratorial voice.

"So, what happened?" asks Emilio.

"I caught a glimpse of Teresa walking in front of the opera house near her home. I didn't approach her. There's no doubt. She is pregnant. It's likely mine."

Emilio finds the strength to remain silent.

"Emilio, I need to know for sure if the child is actually mine. Hospital records, blood samples, eye color, whatever it takes. Can you do that for me? Discreetly?"

"Of course. And, if it is your child, what will you do?"

Intertwining his fingers and locking his hands, Paolo shows resolve rather than nervousness.

"If it's a girl, nothing. If it's a boy, everything."

Chapter 32

Tarquinia, Italy

Renzo spies the young girl with down syndrome in front of the comic book storefront. He just exited the boutique, body shop next door, leaving Ali to converse with the proprietor on matters of esthetic. He needed fresh air, wanting to distance himself from the frank talk of razors and lasers, and feeling pain near the womb. He made Ali laugh by asking if the torturous technique of pubic, laser hair removal was worth the feeling of looking younger, sexier.

The young girl, perhaps 12 years old, stands lost in a trance at the entryway ogling at a particular *fumetto* (comic book)—*Topolino*—a byproduct of Walt Disney's influence on Italian society. The comic book is just steps inside resting on an ad hoc display table. Her knees are scuffed and her hands are a bit dirty. She is pretty with wild, long, blond curls and a sad smile. A tomboy in transition.

Renzo walks past her and picks up the comic book. Looking back, as he makes his way inside the store, he sees the horrified look on the girl's face. Her pupils are dilated. Her fists are clenched. She is traumatized.

Moments later, Renzo exists and sees the young girl sitting at a solitary bistro table on a wooden platform between the two stores. She is lost in tears, staring at the table top.

Not wanting to trigger a flight response in the girl, Renzo grins broadly and walks over to her. He warily places the comic book on the tabletop. Ali, who has exited the beauty shop is watching with wonderment.

"I saw you eyeing this book. It seemed to me that you really wanted it. So, I bought it for you," explains Renzo.

There is a sudden change in the girl's body language. Her expression of surprise and gratitude is unmistakable. She's too shy to speak, no doubt imagining a kind act like this to be part of a dream.

"When I was a little boy I used to come here and look at the comics just like you. A kind man, a neighbor, Giuseppe, would buy me one once in a while. I think it made him happy. I don't think he felt sorry for me. He just wanted me to be happy."

The little girl remains silent.

"Would you accept this from me?" asks Renzo with a big smile.

The little girl nods. She gently grasps the book smiling as she realizes she finally possesses it. With a glint in her eyes, she speeds away, and takes off up *Via Giosuè Carducci* immediately turning right on *Via Umberto* I and out of sight.

Ali sneaks up to Renzo and whispers in his ear.

"If I didn't know better I'd suspect that your random act of kindness was a sly means of making me beg for more sex. Well, it worked. As soon as we get back to the hotel I'm giving you the best sex you've ever had," teases Ali.

Renzo blushes and looks about wondering if there are any listeners.

"I saw her earlier in the park near our car," says Ali. "Those beautiful locks of hair caught my attention. I do think she has the hots for you. After all, girls mature faster than boys."

Renzo's wide-eyed reaction endears Ali.

Holding hands, they trace the young girl's path heading toward the tunnel to their rental car at the perimeter of a cobblestone parkway.

Their white Fiat with two thin red racing stripes is parked two spots away from a stop sign next to the park's retaining stone wall. Ali hesitates and stops to admire a Vespa parked in a restricted place in front of their own vehicle as Renzo proceeds to the Fiat.

"Stop! Stop! Stop!"

The little girl from before is shouting at them from the front of a house next to a *caffetteria* on the other side of the pocket park. She runs as fast as she can toward Renzo. She grabs his wrist and pulls him back to the wall entrance. Ali dumbfounded follows, shouting at the girl.

"What's wrong? What wrong? Are you alright?" Are you in danger?" cries Ali.

The girl picks up two stones along the base of the rotting stone wall and positions herself like a pitcher on a mound. She waits until a van coming up the hill drives by and clears her target. With a full wind-up, she thrusts one stone at the Fiat hitting the hood and ricocheting into the windshield.

Ali is angry.

"What the hell are you doing? Are you crazy?" shouts Ali.

Before Ali or Renzo could react further, the girl whips the second stone and smacks the driver's door handle with a blazing fastball. The force of the Fiat's explosion knocks all three to the ground. Ali hits the pavement but her fall is cushioned by a grassy knoll. Renzo's chest cuffs the end of the Renaissance wall rebounding him to the pavement on his back. The girl seemed to have anticipated the blast and scurries back into the depth of the labyrinth streets of *Tarquinia*.

Renzo collects himself and rushes to Ali. She is alright but too weak to stand.

"Don't move. Wait a moment," consoles Renzo.

Looking at the fireball of flames and smoke engulfing the admired Vespa in front and another vehicle to the rear, Renzo utters words that horrify Ali.

"Cars don't just explode. They may catch fire from a rupture in the fuel line or breach in the fuel tank but cars never explode. Someone connected a bomb activated by opening the driver's door," explains Renzo.

With a harsh tone, Renzo speaks directly, glaring into Ali's face.

"Someone wants me dead."

Ali feels targeted.

"Are you crazy, too? You're blaming me? You think I'm trying to kill you?" cries Ali.

Renzo is mindful.

"Not you. Regina."

Chapter 33

Lido di Tarquinia, Italy

The local *carabinieri* have roped off the crime scene and are taking reports including one from Giuseppina—the mildly handicapped child of the owner of the *caffetteria* across from the parkette. From a distance, she smiles at me. She points a finger to her eyes and waves it over her shoulder. I understand. She saw something before we met. I mouth heartfelt thanks. Standing beside her mother, she beams from ear to ear as she hugs the comic book against her chest.

With our presence no longer needed, Ali hails a passing taxi.

"Ali, I can see that you're upset. I spoke out without thinking. I'm not blaming Regina for this.

Just let me explain," I beg.

"I want to go home. I want to be alone," says Ali to me and then barks an order to the taxi driver, "Take me the Hotel *Miramare* in *Civitavecchia*."

I climb into the waiting taxi alongside Ali. Moments pass. The silence thickens around us. I can hear the sound of the wheels notwithstanding the porous pavement. I alter Ali's plans.

"Driver, forget the hotel. Take us to *il lungomare* (beach) *Tarquinia* and drop us off anywhere along the boardwalk."

Ali pounces.

"No! I told you I want to be left alone."

"We'll get some fresh sea air. Then I'll take you home," I say softly and sincerely.

Ali's shoulders tremble. Her palms are sweating. She rejects my touch and pulls herself away into an anxiety cocoon.

"Ali, it's important that I explain. Later. In private. Regina's misguided beliefs were brought to my attention by Adamo and Anna-Maria. I really don't know what to believe. Is she looking to avenge the honor of your parents?"

Ali ignores my question and loses her temper beyond anything I expected.

"You're a manipulator. Cold and calculating. You present yourself as deeply enlightened but you're not. I know my father was a Mafioso. That's why I left. Regina is an innocent child. Criminality is not hereditary. What you think of her is what you think of me."

"Ali, your mind is jumping from distress to doubt because of the car bomb. Give yourself a chance to focus."

I can see the taxi driver is disturbed by our backseat exchange. He has a look of fearful wonder: what karma has left him with two battling bats in his cab?

"You ring true but you're not true," says Ali. The logic escapes me.

"Ali, you're spinning. I don't know what you're getting at!"

"You're all brain. Your heart emerges only when we make love. You're always calculating, planning, challenging. You're not the little boy of wonder. You're an exploiter. Bottom line: you're wired like all other pig-headed men. Probably worst of the lot because you masquerade your true self so well. I should have paid more attention to the signs."

"What signs? This whole conversation is irrational to me."

"Today, you betrayed me with your words. Previously, you betrayed me with your not so subtle behavior. You keep me away from your friends and family. You break eye contact with me steal glances at passing women. You offer them charming smiles. You interrupt our time together to text your Anna-Maria. You are more emotionally connected to others than to me. I'm certain you've lied to me, if not directly, then by omission. I won't allow anyone to treat me in such a careless and indifferent manner."

I'm taken aback. This must be what a moron feels. I'm throbbing. I'm helpless. I must be going crazy.

"Driver, stop the fucking car!" screams Ali.

The cabbie, frightened by Ali's screeching

command, brings the vehicle to a spinning stop less than a meter from the boardwalk.

"I am not your concubine," shouts Ali drooling from one side of her mouth.

"Ali, I don't know what the hell you're talking about. Where is this all coming from? Calm down and think."

"Go fuck yourself!" spews from her mouth. She takes flight before I have a chance to let her taste my fist.

I look at the driver who is looking back at me. We both turn to watch Ali bolt and run away along the pathway.

We sit in a moment of stunned silence.

"Aren't you going after your woman?" says the cabbie.

I ignore his question and reach over to close the passenger door. I exhale in relief as I nest my head against the headrest. I still in silence. Tearless. Dispassionate.

"*Signore*, what do you want me to do?" asks the driver.

"You can't force a woman to stay in your life. Take me back to *Tarquinia*."

Chapter 34

Lido di Tarquinia, Italy

What's happened to me? I'm a university professor. When did I become a woman scorned? I started with icy silence and now I swear excessively. I dredge up the past and twist its meaning. I storm out dramatically. I lose friends. I don't want to lose my sister too. Regina, where are you?

A large crowd of beach lovers are looking at me as if I'm afflicted with a mental disorder. I subconsciously stray toward Domenico's apartment complex expecting Regina to be there. I'm dizzy and desperately want answers. Is Regina to blame? Was she looking for justice by plotting to kill Renzo? Is she responsible for provoking me? For loading me up with doubts? Are Renzo's words clues that add to my disbelief, my distrust? I want more than signs. I want the unequivocal truth.

I collapse on a park bench next to the *Monumento ai Caduti* (Memorial to Fallen Soldiers). This isn't fatigue. I'm suffering from spiritual stress, bordering on exhaustion, and I'm about to go over the edge. My legs are throbbing. My chest is beating. I feel cracked and I'm tired of talking to myself. What is happening? Perhaps, I shouldn't have come here?

The beach is behind me. A family gathering, perhaps a reunion, is boisterously marking its territory and setting up drinks, paper plates, snacks, and condiments. The young children are digging holes and building sand castles while exhibiting impulsive, defiant hyperactivity. I want to be childfree. I don't want the complications my mother had to face with Regina or me.

Domenico's five-story red brick apartment complex is directly across the street. I can see movement on the top floor. It looks like Regina is standing inside with her back to the open balcony door. She is speaking to a shadow, Domenico no doubt, who is much farther inside the room.

I think of Renzo. Perhaps, I was incoherent. He seemed shocked by everything I said. I should call him. I need to hear his voice.

Locating my cell phone in the depths of my handbag, I press autodial. The phone rings. He doesn't speak. I look at the phone and confirm that we are connected. I explode.

"You prick! You left me at the beach. You didn't even bother to come after me! I was right about you. You are such an asshole. What have you got to say for yourself?"

Renzo doesn't answer me. I look at the phone. We're disconnected.

"The bastard hung up on me," I say out loud.

I redial but there is no answer. I redial again. Again, no answer. I slam my phone against the park bench.

"What's wrong with me. Why did I yell at him?" I say as if talking to someone. In fact, two strangers actively distance themselves from me. They look at me with raised eyebrows.

Suddenly, we are startled by what sounds like a gunshot blast in the air above. I look up and see the shadow lunge for Regina and capture her in a bear hug, twisting and turning. It is Domenico!

I watch them tumble over the edge of the balcony, locked in an embrace, unbroken by the pavement below. Blood pools all around them. I stand and try to shout but not even a murmur comes out.

I feel myself slipping away. I pass out.

PART NINE

"Don't stop thinking about tomorrow." – Fleetwood Mac

Chapter 35

Città di Castel Gandolfo, central Italy

Emilio paces while the four men sit in silence and listen to the special newscast about Mafia activities across Italy. Pope Virgilio is plopped in a white traditional armchair lounge. His crossed hands are holding his black cane that rests between his legs. He looks despondent. Francesco Delacaria, general commander of the *carabinieri*, and his brother, Michele Delacaria, chief investigator on the anti-Mafia commission, rest on a white sofa. Professor Paolo Marin sits in a separate armchair beside the Pope. All the men are focused on the television embedded in the bookshelf across from them. Only Renzo Salvo, sitting in a separate matching armchair with his back to the wall unit, is watching the men, particularly his father.

Various newscasters report on corpses that were dumped on church steps where front entrances were set afire. More corpses were pitched meters from *carabinieri* stations. A hail of machine gun fire at station doors, windows, and parked police cars alerted the police of the corpses. Motorcades were bombed. Most of the dead men are Mafiosi who had broken the code of *omertà* (silence). The Mafia is purging itself of traitors and trumpeting a message to the State and Church: there will be no trust of political elitism and no faith in greedy, self-interested Catholic morality.

The studious atmosphere dissolves when Renzo challenges his father.

"Your silence and isolation was at the cost of innocent lives. Is that what *Stregheria* teaches?"

"Life is a struggle, my son. You cannot let the chariot be torn apart by contesting horses. Social and cultural development cannot be undermined by injustice, corruption and destruction. Sometimes, to restore balance, drastic measures must be taken."

Renzo looks at the tattoo on the inside of his left arm while Pope Virgilio attempts to pacify Renzo but his words lack passion.

"The Mafia scorns religion. Your father is battling a spiritual crisis. *Stregheria* will help the people recapture their roots. What choice do we have? The health of the entire country is at stake!" says Pope Virgilio.

The Delacaria brothers dare not speak. They are good military men torn by the contest of wits.

Renzo, still staring at his father, answers the

Pope's conciliatory remarks.

"You don't have to be religious to be spiritual; nor do you have to believe in God. Some of the best people in history were not religious. Some of the worst crimes have been committed by religious fanatics," states Renzo.

"Oh, cut the crap!" shouts the *Professore* as he jumps to his feet, switches off the television, and commands a counteroffensive against the Mafia.

Renzo listens patiently. The other men are perplexed.

The *Professore* commands a declaration of war against the Mafia. He wants it financed by the coffers of the Vatican bank.

"Let them kill their rank and file. We need to cut off the head of the snake: remove the most dangerous leader and his army will have no direction. This has been a legitimate strategy since the beginning of warfare," declares Paolo.

Renzo, steadfast and authoritative, questions his father's assumptions and directives.

"The situation is much more complex and your motives are suspect," says Renzo who is still seated in his armchair like an emperor on his throne. He remains resolute. His tone is intolerant, harsh and direct.

"You have no love for the Church. Your professed love for *Stregheria* is a ruse to hide your personal crusade against all clergymen. We have already discussed your role in these matters and have decided that it would be best if you remained dead to the world, hiding at the monastery. You will be afforded comfort and discreet luxury," says Renzo.

"What the fuck are you talking about? What do you mean 'we'? Where the hell does Emilio stand on this?" blurts Paolo.

Emilio stops pacing but remains quiet.

"Emilio negotiated an agreement with the American crime families. Now that it's in place, I will negotiate an accord with don Filippo. The counterfeit and selling of fake art, which is spiraling out of control, will cease. It does nothing but dishonor the cultural heritage of Italy. There are abundant Vatican resources, investments and holdings to achieve the combined missions of *Stregheria* and the Church for generations to come. Social programs will flourish. The hypocrisy of the Church, its irregularities and power games, will be confronted. Waste, nepotism, preferential treatment, fraud, money-laundering, unholy investments—will all be scuttled. The Church, to be believed, will return to its roots, *Stregheria*. It will follow the dictates of its own gospel and care for the poor."

"You are playing a dangerous game, my bastard son."

The Pope is struggling to maintain an affable demeanor. The Delacaria brothers stiffen and lean forward in attentiveness. Emilio reverts to pacing. Francesco's hand moves closer to his revolver. Renzo remains absolute.

"Poverty and charity, employment and dignity will be the key words. There is enough money from Peter's Pence alone to finance the renaissance. There will be even more once the mismanagement, privileges, corruption and accounting malpractices are controlled. We control the Papacy but the Mafia controls some cardinals and key politicians. Before we lose total control, we must reform the Curia and weed out Mafia handlers and suppliers from all Vatican operations. We can't do that if we engage the Mafia in an all-out war."

"You have been doing your homework, *bastardo*."

Renzo's calm and confidence is not detoured by his father's name calling.

"You made me the charioteer: a Caesar, not a Roman Senator. For months, I have done nothing but listen and learn. I do not speak ill-prepared. I have had you investigated. While the Church tries to be the white horse, you are the black one seeking to upset the cart."

"You have a talent for drama."

"You forgot to end your sentence with 'bastard'. Yes, I'm your bastard but unlike you, I do not cling to the past. You are a bastard, too. The illegitimate son of a nun and a cardinal."

There is silence. Paolo looks like a tea kettle about to burst with steam. The Pope, profoundly unsettled, begins to rise from his chair as if to part the tension between the two men as the *Professore* pulls a handgun and shoots, hitting the unlucky pope rather than his son.

The scene is charged with kinetic energy and chaotic motion. Michele and Emilio tackle Paolo to the ground and disarm him. Renzo tends to the Pope's wound by applying pressure. As the Swiss guardsman bursts through the door, Francesco fires a bullet into his skull. Through some sort of telepathy, the brothers act in unison. Michele hands over Paolo's gun. Francesco places it in the guardsman's hand.

Francesco provides the answer.

"The guard failed in his attempted assassination of the Pope. Large sums of money were found in his barrack locker, indicating he is a hired killer," offers Francesco.

Emilio, grasping Paolo fiercely, has the last word.

"I will place this tiger back in his monastery cage."

Chapter 36

Palermo, Sicily

Don Filippo mulls over the interesting bit of intelligence presented by Father Alfonso. He stands, walks away and back again, frowning then smiling then shaking his head. He paces to and fro looking frustrated, and then elated. Don Filippo is center stage in the cream-colored social club as he bursts into laughter then takes an angry kick at the air. It's difficult to discern if he is feeling agony or is simply having a heart attack.

Father Alfonso and don Filippo are alone in the *Suttasupra*, a popular meeting place frequented by clan members who want to socialize, play cards, and drink *espresso*. Father Alfonso continues sliding and spinning the stainless-steel rods of the foosball table, and scores a goal against the idle, moveable players.

Don Filippo settles down. In the privacy of the setting, he speaks with ease.

"So, the bastard son survived our bomb and the father continues to feign death. It's time to end our *riposo* (sleep). We have gained from this short rest. The massacre of the Lupo clan and the *carabinieri* crackdown across the south has stamped out the rivals to my leadership. However, we have been stupid. We have taken many lives, young and old, while we fought for territory and supremacy. We have been fighting just to screw each other over. This 'pissing match' ends now. Once again, the Mafia is open for business!" announces don Filippo.

"What do you propose we do?" asks Father Alfonso.

"Luigi, our Tarquinian mole, acted foolishly without support. We can't afford to act rashly. They thwart our objectives and make us look like fucking idiots and broken. We must find the *Professore* and make sure he doesn't cheat death again. Then, we go after his soul; his son, Renzo."

Don Filippo rests his hand on Father Alfonso's shoulder.

"Enough of your priestly duties, I'm placing you in charge. Our soldiers are incompetent. I want you to plan and execute their assassination. Do what you have to do. I will spare no expense. I hold you responsible. Don't disappoint me," says don Filippo.

The men's one-on-one is interrupted by don Filippo's ringing cell phone. He answers with a simple "*Sì*" and listens.

"It's untraceable and it can't be intercepted. What's the message?"

Without saying goodbye, don Filippo pockets the phone. His brow tightens and his weird smile presents an imbalance as if impeded by some orthodontic appliance.

Father Alfonso's interest is piqued.

"What's happened?" asks Father Alfonso.

Don Filippo's look of surprise lingers.

"I'll be damned. A message. Renzo wants to meet me. It seems he has an offer I can't refuse."

Chapter 37

Castel Gandolfo, central Italy

The rhythmic noise of the spinning blades chiselling through the hot morning air is surprisingly unobtrusive.   The convoy of clergy, handlers and dignitaries headed by Renzo wait at a safe distance from the *castel Gandolfo* helipad, chatting amongst themselves, showing scant concern for the descending AugustaWesland AW139 helicopter with its belly lights on.

Seconds after touchdown, Cardinal Fausto—director of the Vatican bank—descends with one civilian and another priest in tow. The downwash of the rotating blades is breezy and helps alleviate the scorching heat of the rising sun. The reception party advances in checkmark formation with

Renzo leading the group. On one side Francesco Delacaria—*Comandate generale dei carabinieri*—is in full regalia while his brother, Michele Delacaria—the chief investigator on the anti-Mafia commission—is impeccable in a corporate blue suit. On the other side, the individuals step back and sidewards patiently waiting to serve as the aircraft ground crew.

Cardinal Fausto marches toward Renzo.

"All yours, my son. No issues encountered," reports Cardinal Fausto.

The Cardinal joins the others in waiting while Renzo and the Delacaria brothers remain to greet the two visitors. Renzo, offering a handshake, is the first to speak.

"Welcome don Filippo. Your acceptance of my invitation is comforting. You being here is a powerful gesture in reducing the violence between our two organizations," claims Renzo.

"Are you kidding me? I wouldn't have missed this for the world," grins don Filippo. "A ride in the Pope's Italian Air Force helicopter to a holy sanctuary and a chance to confront Mr. *Stregheria* himself. Damn you got balls, kid."

Patting his sports jacket, don Filippo carries on.

"Even allowing me to keep my weapon. You're a damn fool or the craftiest enemy I have yet to encounter. I'm betting you're a son of a gun," says don Filippo.

"Right now, I'm hungry. Let's save our surprises and introductions. Please join us inside for brunch. The Pope is waiting for us," says Renzo.

Don Filippo's sidekick interjects.

"Where are the Swiss Guards?" interrupts Father Alfonso.

"Don't be afraid Father Alfonso. The Pope has ordered them to stand down," says Renzo.

"How do you know my name?"

"I know your name and I know what you have done," says Renzo. "You should be more surprised if I didn't."

Chapter 38

Castel Gandolfo, Italy

Abandoning all pretense, don Filippo is direct and crude.

"So, let's get this fucking straight: I back off from the Vatican City and stay planted like the pansies in this garden in my own businesses, and peace will fall from heaven. Is that, right? Nothing is wrong? Just like the Pope is only feeling ill and has a loss of appetite. Not that he is recovering from a wound to his shoulder. A gunshot, perhaps?" says don Filippo with a knowing expression.

Renzo is unruffled refusing to be baited. The men are walking along a private pathway in the *Villa Barberini* gardens that is shaded by opulent oak trees. Renzo halts in front of the ruins of a small

Roman amphitheater. He stares at the ruins.

"Don Filippo, have you ever studied why the Roman Empire fell?"

"Rome was attacked by barbarians. Much like the Mafia now attacking the Vatican, wouldn't you agree?"

Renzo chuckles.

"You do know your history, don Filippo. But that's only part of the story. The Empire overloaded itself with territories and holdings it couldn't afford to manage or maintain. Corruption and political instability were rampant and citizens lost faith in their own leaders and even killed some of them. In that alone, there are lessons for you and I to heed."

"The Vatican, like the Roman Empire, suffers from widespread corruption. Its popularity is crumbling," states don Filippo.

"That, too. However, the Empire's eventual collapse stems from its economic and moral failings. Our disruptive competition is not evolving into something better for either of us. We are merely breaking each other down."

"What's morals got to do with it?" asks don Filippo.

"Are you familiar with Plato's chariot allegory?"

Don Filippo shrugs with boredom. Renzo clarifies.

"A charioteer, driving two winged horses of opposing characters, reins the horses to behave in equilibrium. Peace, order and wealth depend on the charioteer's piloting skills. We are both charioteers, don Filippo. My white horse and your dark horse are inseparable. We need each other. We can't keep biting each other's soul without outside forces ruining us, like this collapsed arena."

"Interesting fairy tale, Renzo, but let's get down to brass tacks as you Americans are so fond of saying. Our agreement is that I continue my Mafia enterprise excluding the drug trade from inside Italy. I will have continued access to make deposits in the Vatican Bank to launder my money, minus your imposed tax of ten percent as a contribution to your social projects."

"Yes."

"There will be families within my network who will not consent to our truce."

"Expected. Together, we will target them and the *carabinieri* will deal with them as always."

Don Filippo's quizzical look is genuine. Finally, he speaks from the heart.

"There are countless riddles in life that erase my doubt that there is a God. His spiritual power answers many mysteries. However, I could never stomach the concept of a Hell. The very idea of pain, misery and punishment for eternity demands a worthy leader. Today, I find myself face to face with the intractable Devil," says don Filippo staring at Renzo.

Renzo remains unimpressed. He continues to look at the greenery. Don Filippo continues.

"I do believe in the power of symbols. You have your twin winged-horses to harness. The Church has its cross to bear. In my case, I have a confederation of families to convince of your sincerity and trust. I need some glue."

"What do you suggest?" asks Renzo.

"It's not a suggestion. It's a make it or break it offering. I want Paolo, your father."

Renzo turns to face don Filippo square on, exhibiting the first signs of flushing and anger.

"Done. My father can rote in Hell."

Chapter 39

Monastery at Lake Como, Bellagio, Northern Italy

"There is no need to apologize," says the bent, gray-haired priest. "I am hours away from sleep. We are all holy men serving God. You will find this cell comfortable as are all others in the dormitory. It is very clean and tidy and there are fresh towels and plenty of hot water. It's easy to lose track of time in our countryside and find yourself betwixt, uncertain to go forward or back. Where are you travelling to?"

Father Alfonso smiles but ignores the question and quotes the Bible.

"The Lord keeps you from all harm and watches over your life."

"Ah, so true, Psalm 121:7-8 which concludes, T*he Lord keeps watch over you as you come and go,* *both now and forever."*

The priest opens one of the window curtains to reveal a crisp half-moon.

"Feel free to walkabout. The cloister walk links to the refectory and beyond with the library. At the very end, there is a barn and a garden with an unbelievable, if I'm permitted to use that word, view of the lake and town. It is a refreshing place for prayer under first morning light."

Changing the subject, Father Alfonso asks about an old friend.

"I am told, by his family, that Father Giancarlo resides here. We were boyhood friends in *Spormaggiore*. I was assigned there briefly one summer under his tutelage."

"Yes, he is here. Unfortunately, he is senile. It's very sad really. He keeps his physical strength but his cognitive abilities suffer. He splits his time, day and night, between the barn and the library. He does nothing in either except look, read and try to remember. He will not recognize you, I'm afraid."

"I only wish to offer reassurance."

"Of course. May I suggest that you speak slowly with him and don't pose questions. Speak to him in short sentences and let him read your eyes."

"Excellent advice. Thank you."

"Goodnight, Father. May God be with you."

"And, with you."

The old priest disappears down the covered walkway. Father Alfonso, under cover of his hooded black cloak, sneaks along the path in the opposite direction. Only two priests, seated well apart, are in the dining hall. One is reading. The other is sipping a drink. Father Alfonso looks about but he has no interest here. He bypasses the library and heads straight for the barn. In the moonlight, he hunches to cast a low shadow of himself. Inside the barn, he spots a claw hammer. He hides the hammer inside the sleeve of his robe and walks back, hands tucked inside opposite sleeves, in a slow stroll as if absorbed in contemplation.

The meditative façade is discarded as soon as he reaches the library door. He sees his target and walks in.

Professor Paolo Marin impersonates Father Giancarlo with ease. He offers a slight nod followed by a look of bewilderment, then a shrug as Father Alfonso enters the room. Father Alfonso browses. The professor feigns reading under the light of an antique, solid porcelain lamp with a cherub angel shade. Periodically, he stands then sits, then stands, as if struggling with psychic demons.

Father Alfonso tires of the dance. He walks directly in front of the upright Paolo and invades his space.

"So, you are Father Giancarlo?" asks Father Alfonso rhetorically.

Swiftly and forcefully, Paolo propels the lamp across the side of Father Alfonso's face dropping him to the floor rendering him immobile. The hammer has slipped out of Alfonso's sleeves, out into the open. Paolo picks it up and wields it against both of the prone man's knee caps who recoils even in his unconsciousness.

"My name is professor Paolo Marin, alias Father Giancarlo. You think I don't know who you are? Whereas I have always found you an irritant to my cause, Father Alfonso, my blood pressure surges for those who have betrayed me. Only my best friends and my bastard son know of my seclusion. First I take care of you. Then, I'll kill them."

Paolo is moving slowly and confidently winding his way down the pathway. He is the only traveler descending the hill in the thickness of darkness. At the summit behind him, a small fire turns into a fiery blaze. Father Alfonso is ablaze at the base of a crude burning, wooden cross. His horrifying screams echo in the night, rousing the living and the dead from their serenity.

Chapter 40

Spormaggiore, northern Italy

"Call your husband. Tell him you need him. Tell him you want to make love to him and to hurry home," demands Paolo.

Grazia is distraught, on the verge of a mental collapse. Her forehead is soiled by blood from a blow. Her dry, frazzled hair contrasts with her swollen, shiny and teary eyelids and cheeks. She is sitting on the end of a sofa with Paolo perched on the coffee table in front of her. She can't stop crying.

"I don't want to go upstairs and wake one of your children. Don't force me," warns Paolo.

The transparent threat flings Grazia in hysterics which Paolo immediately douses with yet another whip of the gun's butt across Grazia's face.

The strike is brutal. Paolo is crazed. Any semblance of civility has vanished. The dormant evil within him has sprung to the surface with a startling desire for payback.

In her state of semi consciousness, Grazia pleads.

"Please don't hurt my children."

Paolo grips Grazia's chin, forcing her to look up at him. He reissues his command.

"Call him," commands Paolo.

"Friends invited him to *Baita Marnara* for a trout dinner. I don't know if he's still there," cries Grazia.

Paolo picks up the phone receiver on the end table and hands it to her. He dials the number, knowing the restaurant well. Grazia, cupping her brow with her left hand, holds the receiver against her right ear. She is struggling to maintain consciousness. Paolo presses the gun barrel into her stomach.

"Hi, Susanna? Yes, it's Grazia. Please let me talk to Emilio. What? Yes, yes, I'm fine. Ciao."

Looking at Paolo, Grazia begins crying again.

"He's already on his way home," says Grazia.

Catching her composure, Grazia begs.

"Why are you doing this? You are family. Everyone thought you were killed in a car accident. We prayed for you. What is happening?"

"Shut the fuck up!"

Only minutes pass in the hostage crisis before footsteps are heard coming up the wooden steps to the front door. Paolo, standing behind the couch, swings his hand to muffle Grazia's mouth and digs the gun into the top of her head.

Emilio keys the lock and enters. He steps forward and is shocked by the surreal image. He doesn't recognize his wife at first, nor Paolo. Reality slaps him hard. He snaps at Paolo.

"Paolo! What the hell are you doing?" yells Emilio.

As Emilio step forward to help his wife, Paolo shoots him. The bullet penetrates Emilio's lower right shoulder, throwing him backward against the wall. He ricochets forward and falls on his knees. With one hand on his wound, he sees his kids standing at the top of the stairs. Three white ghosts spooked by loud voices and gunfire. They're frozen in shock at the sight of their blood splattered father and tortured mother.

Grazia breaks loose and dashes up the stairs to shield her children. Paolo lets her go and takes a step closer to Emilio. Paolo aims and shoots Emilio again in the stomach. Grazia screams uncontrollably, gripping her crying children in a fearful bear hug. Emilio's is a twisted, grotesque lump next to the coffee table. He is breathless.

"One down, more to come," says Paolo.

Paolo escapes like an adulterer on the run. He purposely empties the remaining rounds into the lit windows of neighboring homes to discourage gawkers and good Samaritans.

Ozzie Logozzo

PART TEN

"I know, it's everybody's sin, you gotta lose to know how to win." - Aerosmith

Chapter 41

Tarquinia, central Italy

"Anna-Maria likes you. It's not my imagination. She's sensuous, smart. Quite spellbinding, don't you think?" says mamma Teresa trying to play the matchmaker.

"Yes, she is very smart...and beautiful," responds Renzo who is unable to hide his embarrassment.

Renzo continues to hesitate as mamma Teresa smiles. He is uncertain as to what to do with himself. He fumbles with the cookie tray and stuffs *biscotti* in his mouth to avoid further talk.

"I think she's the perfect woman, virtuous, vibrant, vivacious. She's perfect for you."

Coughing through his chewing, Renzo

manages a remark.

"I think I'm still married. No papers have arrived from Emily as of yesterday."

"That's just a technicality. The mail is slower than the fastest snail. But you can really tell you're an American. You cling to the old ways. Here in Italy we've become much more liberal. You know, you don't have to remarry. Just live together. Everyone needs to be loved. Especially, you and Anna-Maria."

Renzo is surprised by Mamma Teresa's openness. His discomfort intensifies as Anna-Maria returns from mamma's kitchen with a pot of *espresso*. Her face is flushed. Obviously, she overheard the exchange. Although she redirects the dialogue, she sits on the couch next to Renzo drawing a smile from mamma who is pacing in front of her balcony door.

"Emilio has survived Paolo's attack but he remains hospitalized," reports Anna-Maria. "The doctors believe that with aggressive physiotherapy and a strong will, there is a good chance that he will walk again. It will be several more months before we get a definitive diagnosis."

Mamma looks at the clear, blue sky. Speaking to her son, she sighs.

"Just when you gained don Filippo's acquiescence we have your father run afoul of his senses. Emilio's commitment to Paolo was undeniable. He was forever grateful for the financial help for his brothers' education, for securing them positions within the Vatican and, no doubt, for savings his own sorry ass from the cuckold and his shotgun. Being a part of the *carabinieri* was the best thing that ever happened to him. Hopefully his past training will help him recover from Paolo's psychotic attack."

Unafraid to speak frankly even in front of Anna-Maria, mamma Teresa addresses her son's own dilemma.

"You're too much intellect, not enough emotion. You don't like rejection. That's why you didn't face Emily at the airport. You let Emilio be your proxy," says mamma Teresa.

"It wasn't the first time a woman scorned me," snaps Renzo.

Renzo's remark is like a dagger to mamma's heart. She's deflated, speechless. Her eyes water. Anna-Maria intercedes.

"You can't let your past hurt your present. Perhaps all those years you stayed with Emily because you feared further rejection. I don't know," says Anna-Maria as she places her hand on Renzo's thigh. "You chose to remain with us. To become our new leader. There's no reason not to love again."

Anna-Maria's unexpected boldness comforts Renzo.

"I like the basic principles of *Stregheria*. It aligns with many of my own beliefs. I decided to stay because there wasn't a reason to go back. Discovering that Emily was my cousin, however distant, actually gave me hope that it would bring us closer together. I don't think she cared that we were cousins. Others certainly didn't. However, she crossed the line with her unfaithfulness. There is no going back for me," says Renzo with finality in his voice.

Mamma, no longer comfortable with the discourse, refocuses on the problem of Paolo.

"What about Paolo? What do we do? How are we going to find him?"

Renzo repositioning his coffee cup back on his saucer and placing it on the table responds.

"You don't have to worry about that."

Looking at his mother, Renzo pries her memory.

"Do you remember when once when we went to mass together? I was five years old. I wanted to taste the Eucharist. You slapped the back of my head."

Mamma smiles faintly.

"I still remember the phrases, perhaps not accurately, the priest used in his sermon. He said, 'When you feel lost, God will find you'. So, too, will Paolo," says Renzo.

Anna-Maria interjects the last words.

"Darkness and tragedy are twins. Let's hope Paolo's madness mellows before he buries us all."

Chapter 42

Frankfurt, Germany

"Sebastiano, I really don't know if the managers of the Vatican Bank were grossly incompetent or embezzlers bent on extravagant spending or simply stupid souls. It's a sad saga of shady deals, scandals and smokescreens," says Renzo.

Sebastiano, as if personally found guilty of a misdemeanor, lowers his head in national shame.

"I have looked at the Vatican records. Billions were hidden in its walls during wartime. Money that actually belonged to the Jews. The Vatican knew of the Holocaust before anyone else. The Church helped Nazi war criminals even after the war," says Renzo with arms open, hands out in front.

Sebastiano shrugs his shoulders. He voices the agreed upon strategy.

"It's appalling. Right now, however, the Mafia's money and the squandering of donations by clergy is our concern. We may not be able to recover past personal expenses but we will put a stop to the spending on cars, luxury apartments, mistresses, and their extravagant life style. We will freeze their accounts. Many priests will go into default. Many Mafiosi will be compelled to donate a portion of their funds to our cause," says Sebastiano.

Renzo and Sebastiano are seated at an outside table at the *Steigenberger Frankfurter Hof*, a hotel in the heart of the financial district and a few minutes' walk around the corner from their seven o'clock appointment at the *VolkzBank*.

The flagship hotel with an excess of pillars and arches is blazing with decorative lighting. The restaurant in the inner courtyard has a serene ambience. Glowing candles on tabletops and on iron floor candle holders proliferate. Renzo and Sebastiano are under an open patio umbrella indulging in pastry and coffee.

"This Kraut coffee has no *panna* on top. The aroma is lost. The barista should be fired."

"Sebastiano, don't look at me for validation. I still prefer to linger over my *espresso macchiato* unlike your two second swallow."

Changing the topic, Sebastiano treads on sensitive ground.

"I will never forget my first love," confesses Sebastiano. "She was the perfect partner. She awakened feelings in me I had never had before, mostly pain. It hurts me still. I was innocent. She was so mature. Yet, I thought we could make it work. I still think about what could have happened if I only could make her fall in love with me," concludes Sebastiano with a hopeless, clownish expression.

Renzo, touched by Sebastiano's disclosure, reciprocates with inner thoughts of his own.

"I'm not certain I ever experienced love. There were many days I didn't want to go home. I got so tired of being compared to other men, the omissions, the outright lies. My lover complained and ranted to others, divulging personal matters. Intimate discussions should not be newsreel. It destroys the love. It shifts platonic friendships into flirting and adultery. You can't heal a marriage with a malicious mouth," says Renzo with clenched fists.

"Renzo, even during my first love, I'd find myself checking out attractive women. Do you think I'm foolish?"

"Sebastiano, you're asking me to define infidelity. My wife had a constant need to point out that my view was socially inept. Maybe so but I don't think flirting is harmless. I think infidelity begins when you give more emotional attention to another than to your own partner. You're cheating as soon as that happens. It inevitably leads to intimate conversations, hugging, kissing, lies and physical transgressions."

"But I see you look at other women. Aren't you checking them out?" asks Sebastiano with a genuine interest in Renzo's viewpoint.

"I guess I am but I look at people regardless of their bodies. We all have the same body parts.

Some are fit, many are fat. The only difference is faces. Study the face and you'll glimpse the person's soul. Isn't that what philosophers tell us?"

"Is that why you still have feelings for Emily? You saw something inside her she didn't recognize in herself."

"Perhaps or perhaps, I just imagined it."

Renzo swigs the balance of his coffee.

"We don't want to be late for our appointment. Let's go," says Renzo.

The men rise and walk onto the sidewalk crossing the street.

"Tell me, Sebastiano, does your first love still live in *Tarquinia*?"

"Oh, goodness, no. In Naples, maybe. It was Sophia Loren," chuckles Sebastiano.

Renzo stops in his tracks as an approaching vehicle honks at him. He gives Sebastiano a friendly smack to the back of his head and an apologetic wave to the driver. Sebastiano offers an everlasting, innocent smile.

The private institute is a leading international commercial bank with many subsidiaries largely dealing with corporate clients and institutional investors. It generates gross revenues each year in excess of ten billion Euros. The three-story cornerstone structure is rock-solid with ground level, eighteen-feet arched windows and entrance secured by thick wrought iron grillwork. A single light illuminates the second story end unit where the curtain is fluttering with the breeze from the open window.

Sebastiano taps on the glass door pane.

Immediately, the door opens.

"I was waiting wondering why you are late."

Renzo takes the lead.

"Mr. Weber, we apologize. It's the Italian style. Sebastiano here had me engrossed in an engaging story of love and betrayal."

"Please, call me Yogesh. Let's go to my study upstairs. I have coffee and cake for us."

Sebastiano makes a nauseated face. They follow Yogesh dutifully.

Yogesh's study is atypical. The place is littered with paperwork, reading material, files, books and computer printouts. The room has a functional fireplace and wainscoting but the focal piece is a six-chair, executive table with a silver platter of assorted pastries and a decanter of coffee. A large projection screen is mounted on the wall.

Sebastiano repositions the catered goodies to one side and unzips his portfolio and plants a folder marked 'Yogesh Weber' in front of the banker. Renzo sits at the head of the table as if he's an independent, impartial adjudicator while Yogesh sits across Sebastiano.

Sebastiano takes the lead. Renzo stares at Yogesh without expression.

"Let's not dally, Mr. Weber. Your bank has deposits from several of our Church officials," begins Sebastiano.

Sebastiano extracts a printout from his folder and passes it to Yogesh for inspection and continues with his exposition.

"The list dates back to events that transpired during World War II. Several of our clerics, including the Archbishop Werner Marin, abdicated their moral position and engaged in profiteering. Most of those deposits were in cash. Cash that was carried across the border in suitcases. Portions of that money represent donations, 'Peter's Pence' specifically, and another sizeable serving is derived from money laundering, particularly political dealings, tax evasions and criminal activity. The most interesting assets stem from life insurance policies of deceased Jewish policyholders. In all such instances, the insurance companies refused to issue compensation to policy holders without proof of death certificates, knowing full well that such evidence was unattainable."

Sebastiano fully opens the file folder and spreads out the remaining papers and photographs. Yogesh's face blanches. His hands begin to tremble. Sebastiano gets to the most telling point of his revelations.

"You Yogesh Weber, born Burnard Bamberger, served as a board member of the Council of Economic Advisors for the insurance companies. These documents reveal your leading role in policy and investment decisions. The most revealing items are highlighted in these photos. You acted as a doctor in the SS Medical Corps. Your Nazi duties involved carrying out the selection of so-called 'inferior humans': euthanasia, sterilization, infectious disease research, and a variety of indescribable human experiments. There's more. So much more," says Sebastiano fully enjoying discrediting the banker.

Yogesh, looking distraught, asks the obvious.

"What do you want?" asks Yogesh. Sebastiano answers.

"Simply your co-operation. There are several accounts that rightly belong to the Vatican. All those will be transferred to Mr. Renzo Salvo, in trust for the Vatican Bank. That's it. Nothing else. You can keep everything else including your freedom."

"But we are talking about billions of Euros," exclaims Yogesh.

"Yes, we are. We can tell you exactly how much to the Euro," says Sebastiano.

Finally, Renzo leans forward wanting to have the last word.

"We will have that money, with you or without you. We are offering you an irrevocable deal to partner up with us. You have one minute to decide," says Renzo, speaking confidently.

Yogesh, brooding, looks at the two men and then at the family protrait on the wall. Thirty seconds of silence pass. Finally, Yogesh stands, gets his computer and turns on the projection screen and speaks.

"So be it."

Chapter 43

Marina di Gioiosa Ionica, Calabria

The municipality of *Marina di Gioiosa Ionica* in the Italian region of Calabria is purgatory: a temporal town teeter-tottering between punishment and pardon, where most people repent their transgressions and ache for God's forgiveness.

Its wide, sandy beaches and crystal clear sea, decree rest and recreation. It is a place where the land and the sun's energy support family ties. A place where living a simple life dates back to the Greek colonization of the area before the Roman Empire.

Family is the most important thing in the culture of the region. However, some families in this area are quite different. They are not therapeutic or wholesome units. They are crime families.

The recent catastrophe in this Calabrian town perpetuates a nauseating sense of stagnation—physical and mental. Many folks struggle to forget the horrors. Many families fear more calamities in the once peaceful paradise.

Corrado Lupo, *capo di tutti i capi* (boss of all bosses), and his Mafia minions had ruled *Gioiosa*. From the funeral home, *San Giovanni Camera Mortuaria*, a terminal for body laundering, and from *la chiesa di San Nicola* (St. Nicholas Church), a block away but connected by an underground tunnel, the don ran his Mafia empire.

What has been reported as Mafia gang conflicts for control of the lucrative drug trade gave rise to sabotage, beatings, assassinations, bombings, and retaliations. However, none of the incidents throughout southern Italy compare to the unheard-of brutality and the annihilation that occurred in *Gioiosa*.

One night, forever etched in the collective memory, explosions ignited the sky. Gunfire, blasts and fireballs filled the air. Men, women and children were maimed, burned alive, dismembered and killed. The church, the funeral home and numerous buildings in the surrounding area were reduced to ashes. Waves of devastation spread from this epicenter: ruptured water pipes, broken gas and electrical lines, burning trees and houses.

During the Armageddon, don Corrado, family and friends were exterminated. The nation was horrified. The politicians pontificated. The papacy pitched prayer. Doublespeak and ambiguity filled the airwaves but nothing really changed except for the worse.

There are no plans for reconstruction. Bitterness towards government and the Church intensifies. Talk of a mafia resurgence is spreading.

A lone resident, holding brass altar bells, stands at the site of the devastation. No birds come to sing in the vicinity. Every Sunday since the disaster, this old man has carried his limp body to the consecrated grounds to signal for the Lord's blessing.

Today's ritual is different. The bells are ringing in his hand without assistance. His entire body is rattling. The panic in his face echoes a song of Sirens, winged maidens of the Earth, calling out to the community. Folks peer out of windows, balconies and doorways. Many run into the streets dizzy with fright. They feel tremors. The ground is moving. One woman screams "*Sirens* are calling us to our death" prophesizing doomsday like the mythical Cassandra.

The vision is blurry but from *Strada Torre Vecchia* a cavalcade of light rays reflecting off the shiny steel surfaces advances. Everyone looks up but it is like staring at the sun; the light is blinding. The noise of a convoy of dump trucks, bulldozers, excavators, front loader tractors, tower cranes and other heavy machinery is escalating.

The apocalyptic invasion of the machines stops short of ground zero. No resident dares to move. A motorcade passes into the clearance. *Carabinieri* ride BMW motorcycles and drive armored SUVs. There is also a Lotus and a Lamborghini.

Strangely, a modest Fiat 500 breaks rank from the security fleet and stops in front of the bell-ringer. The driver steps out to open the back door. The Pontiff emerges with a sorrowful smile.

Everyone is frozen in time. There is no movement except for Pope Virgilio approaching the old man and his bells. The Pope reaches for the old man's hand. He kisses it tenderly then turns to address the people. A *carabiniere* holds a megaphone up for the Pope's convenience. The Pope speaks.

"I am so sorry. I want us to remember the sins and forgive the sinners. I feel your pain and suffering. These immoralities are grave but we must remain humble and forgive. 'Vengeance is mine, I will repay' says the lord. The word of the Lord endures forever. Amen," says the Pope sadly.

A collective 'Amen' resounds from the crowd.

Looking at the gathering and pointing at a lone figure stationed in front of the Fiat 500, Pope Virgilio promises good news.

"My dear friend and emissary, Renzo Salvo, will speak to you of the rebirth, the renaissance of this treasured *Marina di Gioiosa Ionica*," says the Pope to Renzo. "But first, let us celebrate mass."

PART ELEVEN

"There's a killer on the road." – The Doors

Chapter 44

Trento University, Trento, 3a.m.
'In the beginning'

The knock on the school hallway door is authoritative.

"It's open," says *professor* Paolo with an air of annoyance.

A pretty, young woman possessing a manner of independence enters, broadcasting a winning smile. Her demeanor is poised and polished, much more than the typical ungroomed, bookish co-eds who lack style.

Paolo, the lord of the manor, seems distracted. His stare is invasive, threatening.

"You're late. You made me wait a long time. I don't like to wait," declares Paolo.

"It couldn't be helped," says the woman

unapologetically.

"Where's Ebony?" asks Paolo.

"Serena is on her period and feeling terribly sick," says the woman unemotionally.

"You know I prefer lots of lust and that the customer is always right," says Paolo without any attempt to hide his lewdness.

"You did sound desperate on the phone so I brought you a surprise, if you can afford it," says the woman in an attempt to playfully provoke Paolo into a better mood.

"Really? Money has never been a problem," says Paolo.

The woman smiles and returns to the door. She motions to someone to come in. Two other ladies carrying oversized satchels file in like social butterflies, smiling and giggling.

Paolo asks the ringleader.

"Gemma, are they virgins?" says Paolo beaming a pleased expression. Paolo comes around from his desk and faces the two women standing in front of the sofa. He gets closer to the duo and repeats "Very nice," several times.

"Yes. Now sit down on the couch and let us prepare," says Gemma as she pushes Paolo into the corner of the sofa. He offers no resistance.

"Do you have the money for three of us?" asks Gemma wanting to first take care of business.

"Of course, I do."

"Payment up front, please."

Paolo retrieves his wallet in the face of Gemma's outstretched palm. He plants six large bills in her hand.

"Make sure you're and your companions are worth it. Surprise me and if you succeed I give you all three times as much," Paolo promises.

One of the ladies proceeds to the back of the sofa and begins to blindfold Paolo.

"We have a magical ritual for you. Sex is energy and we will create enough pleasure to banish your inner demons," says Gemma.

"I doubt it. My desire for revenge is overpowering. Don't add to it by keeping me waiting long. I've had enough already."

The ladies busy themselves with preparations. The door is locked. The window blinds are drawn. Candles are lit and mellow, classical music is playing on the radio. Paolo's hands are raised behind his head, roped, tied and anchored to the back of the sofa's leg. A few more moments of commotion end with Paolo's blindfold being removed by Gemma.

"Do you like it?" asks Gemma.

The three women are facing Paolo. Each is fully naked draped in a black sheer cape buttoned only at the collar.

"It's not bad at all," says Paolo, "but so far it's all sizzle and no steak. Prove your worth."

"It will be our pleasure," laughs Gemma, cuing the other women to converge on Paolo and begin the orgy.

Chapter 45

Vatican City, Italy
'In the beginning'

The doctor withdraws the lit candle held next to the mouth of the Pope. The flame does not flicker. He takes out his stethoscope from his bag and listens for a heartbeat. There is nothing from the Pope who lies motionless on his bed. Through the darkness of the room, the doctor looks at the small assemblage in the Pope's chamber.

"The Pope is dead," he pronounces.

Everyone falls to their knees in prayer.

After kissing the pontiff's hand, Father Virgilio, the *Camerlengo* (chamberlain) entrusted with the property and revenues of the Holy See, and Father Pio, head of the Board of Superintendence of the Vatican Bank, a post previously held by their mentor, Werner Marin, exchange knowing smiles which others in the chamber interpret as gladness for the Pope's death. As mentees they have been patient, working their painstaking plans and guided machinations for this eventuality. Within weeks, the College of Cardinals will meet in Rome for the conclave to elect a new pope. The selection of a successor will be controlled notwithstanding the secret balloting.

"I will summon the enclave and prepare the funeral rites. Father Pio, please walk with me. We need to discuss embalmment and the funeral mass."

Once in the hallway, Father Virgilio turns to his brother.

"It's best we discuss our next steps beyond the Vatican walls. We need privacy and discretion. Let's lunch at our usual place on *via Borgo Pio*," whispers Father Virgilio.

The brothers walk across Saint Peter's square heading toward the *Colonnato del Bernini*. The pace is leisurely; time is not of the essence. They stroll down *Via dei Corridori*, away from the hordes of tourists, alongside the wall without disturbance. Once at *Il Passetto di Borgo*, they head for the *ristorante*.

Il Ristorante Tre Pupazzi is one of several eateries in the area. Priests, known for their finicky eating habits, frequent this establishment. Virgilio and Pio, habitual visitors, have befriended the owner who greets them and treats them like family.

"*Benvenuto*, welcome," says the portly proprietor.

Hearty handshakes are exchanged. The

owner who is also the chef wears a blue soccer tee shirt, a red apron and a genuine, spectacularly jovial expression. He escorts them to their favorite table butting off the side wall where there hangs a photograph of the now deceased Pope. Interestingly, the photo is dwarfed by a set of oversized fork, knife and spoon hung above the adjacent table. Father Pio can't resist a reference to the juxtaposition between food and religious art that dominates the *ristorante*.

"Food before religion. We Italians have our priorities, right?" laughs Father Pio.

There is no need to place an order. While the daily specials are prepared, chef and sons bring two carafes of homemade red and white wine along with a platter of various cheeses and *bruschetta*.

"Make sure you drink and eat everything. Don't worry we'll carry you back if we have to," jokes the proprietor.

After a bit of banter, the priests are left to their own devices.

"Pio, is it my imagination or does it seem that Paolo wasn't really moved by the death of his father last month?" asks Father Virgilio.

"I didn't really take notice. He may be a clown on the soccer field but when it comes to relationships he is very quiet and introspective," says Father Pio.

"Yes, yes. But, I have reservations…Not about scheming to make me Pope," clarifies Father Virgilio who looks about before continuing his confession.

"I don't know if *Stregheria* is the right answer. I've long doubted Paolo's intentions. I think he's got more skin in the game than he cares to reveal to us…

some hidden motives," says Father Virgilio.

"Maybe so but so what. Look what he has done for our family. Our pipeline to the Vatican Bank is unassailable. Our Frankfurt accounts are untouchable and, before month's end, you will be pope."

"You've made all the arrangements?" asks Father Virgilio.

"Of course. There will be little need to network for votes with the cardinals. A difficult task since they are scattered throughout the Vatican. We will control the enclave. The dean of the College of Cardinals will supervise the proceedings. The names of nine voting cardinals will be chosen at random. In truth, all nine have been preselected. Agreements and commitments have been stressed with each one of them. Our friends will keep their privileges and their German bank accounts will be left untouched as long as they follow our direction," emphasizes Father Pio.

Leaning forward, Pio whispers the remaining preparations.

"Three will collect the votes of any sick cardinals, three will serve as scrutineers, and three others will check the work of the scrutineers. After the casting of the ballots, each scrutineer will examine each ballot while the last scrutineer will call out your name ignoring the one on the ballot until we have two-thirds of the votes. The revisers will presumably check for any errors and then the ballots will be burned immediately. Your election will be announced after the first ballot. We do not want first-vote ballots sitting idle on a plate until the conclusion of a second vote. The election of the pontiff shall be swift," says Father Pio.

"The day is finally here, Pio. What we wildly imagined. A lot of fat ladies in the square will sing with the rise of the white smoke," says Father Virgilio with a look of wonderment.

"From pauper to Pope. Pope Virgilio, you make a brother proud."

"Thanks to Werner, rest his soul, and to Paolo," says Father Virgilio. "Although I have reservations about *Stregheria*, I will make Paolo our trusted advisor. Perhaps I can mellow his mission. If not, the Church and *Stregheria*, will be at war."

Chapter 46

Tarquinia, Italy

Like a chimpanzee who kills his neighbors to protect his territory or to gain dominance, Paolo, high on adrenaline, is on the hunt to kill his errant son.

It's nightfall in *Tarquinia*. It's too early for a café snack and communal chat with friends; and not late enough for a post-meal *passeggiata* (stroll) in the *piazza*. Shops are closed. The sky is gloomy. There aren't any pedestrians walking the streets. Staff in the bars and restaurants are in kitchens preparing evening meals. Families and friends are at home together, discoursing the day's distresses and successes. It is starting to rain giving Paolo sole possession of the side streets leading to mamma

Teresa's apartment.

Paolo seeks sanctuary under the tunnel archway that faces *Viale Luigi Dasti* and *Piazzale Europa*. A portion of the parkette, the site of a recent car bombing, remains cordoned off by the *carabinieri*. Crossing the parkette is the quickest and least conspicuous route to mamma Teresa's apartment on *Via IV Novembre*. Gawkers have long since disappeared as have superstitious souls who fear lightning might strike twice.

The rain has shifted to a downpour. Caught in the shower, Paolo has no desire to wait until it's spent. He steps swiftly out of the old town onto the parkette grounds, along the darkness of the back perimeter to avoid the corridor of street lamps. A very old lady seated on a park bench is awakened by the rainstorm and intermittent thunderclap. Her visibility is completely trashed. She rises and finds her way, lured by the strong smell of cooked tomatoes and arugula wafting from a gated home across the cobblestone street. Her gait is bent. Her pace is painfully labored. She's soaked like meat that's been marinated overnight.

Paolo's feet slosh through puddles as he emerges at the far end and runs across the intersection, resting momentarily under a large tree in the roundabout. Constantly looking around himself, he jogs to the bus stop canopy. He is nearly in total darkness. There are no more street lights in his path and no moonlight. He checks his inside pocket for his gun. Deftly, he drops the old *Beretta* magazine to the ground, grabs another round and loads it into his handgun. He doesn't care what telltale litter he leaves behind.

Avoiding open space, Paolo, drenched and physically distorted from bodily aches, prowls along the apartment building's iron gate until he reaches the driveway to the underground garage. He hops onto a garbage bin positioned against the stone wall. He scales the wall and gingerly walks along its ledge until he reaches the back of the building.

The single, steel glass door is locked. It is made of tempered glass. Paolo, timing his strikes to the thunderbolts, uses his gun to smash the door handle and lock repeatedly without success. The molding along the door's sidelights is compromised by age. Its exposed wood frame construction is failing. Paolo whips his pistol at the jamb like an adult carpenter bee digging a tunnel through the frame. His frenzy is frightening. With one final crazed foot stomp, a chunk of wood paneling is dislodged but his ankle is lacerated from the shattered glass. He reaches in to unlock the door. Once inside, he sits on the back stairs, pulls out a shard of glass that was embedded in his ankle and laces the swelling wound with his handkerchief. Blood continues to drip, nonetheless.

Anguished and winded, Paolo tackles the service stairwell up to the top floor. With each foot forward, he shows signs of fatigue and breathlessness. At last, he reaches his destination. The exit door flanks the elevator shaft. Someone is coming. He is standing directly in front of the elevator. As the compartment comes to a halt, he makes direct eye contact with Anna-Maria. She is startled by Paolo's gruesome appearance. Paolo points his gun through the ornate, metal birdcage door. Anna-Maria remains motionless as Paolo opens the door and waves at her to come out. She obliges.

Paolo lodges his firearm at the base of Anna-Maria's skull and pushes her toward mamma Teresa's apartment door. She knocks.

Adamo's voice is heard from inside.

"Anna-Maria, come on in. It's open," says Adamo.

Paolo's left hand collars his hostage. The gun is pressing against Anna-Maria's right cheek.

"He's got a gun!" Anna-Maria cries.

The beauty and the deranged beast enter. Paolo has Anna-Maria's neck in an armlock.

Adamo, armed with a *Beretta* 92, draws it and aims, holding the weapon with both hands. Sebastiano, mamma Teresa, and Renzo, startled, are beside themselves. Renzo intervenes.

"Both of you, lower your guns! We are family," declares Renzo.

Adamo fixated on his target responds first.

"I'm doing no such thing. Put the gun down or I'll blow you past Hell's gates," asserts Adamo.

"A kid with imagination. You raised him good, Teresa. Too bad he's not mine like this other prick. Or, maybe that's a good thing," says Paolo.

Teresa begs, "Please Paolo, put the gun down. Let's talk this out."

Renzo steps forward, "Your quarrel is with me. Don't involve innocent people. Let Anna-Maria go."

Obliging, Paolo thrusts Anna-Maria into

Renzo's arms and aims the gun right at Teresa's face.

"So, Adamo, you want to be the cause of your mother's death? Go ahead pull the trigger. We'll both go down in loving memory," taunts Paolo.

Adamo's focus is unbroken. He keeps his fear and panic at bay.

"My ungrateful son has deposed me. He's turned me into a cold-blooded killer. I'm crazy? Yes. Because of him," says Paolo.

"I didn't ask for your role. You schemed to put me in charge. You can't expect me to be your lap dog," challenges Renzo.

Sebastiano is slowly maneuvering out of Paolo's peripheral vision inching towards mamma Teresa's steel walking stick perched next to the console table.

"Touch it and mamma wouldn't need it anymore," asserts Paolo.

Sebastiano surrenders. His shoulders droop in helplessness.

Paolo continues, "The Bible says, 'Thou shall not kill', yet Christians are magnificent killers. It would be madness not to kill each other. It's better than a living death. Don't you agree, Teresa?"

Mamma Teresa shows understanding and empathy.

"Paolo, your Church did not punish or kill your mother. Humans did that to themselves. Your mother and father hurt each other. Your father abandoned your mother. I abandoned you," says mamma Teresa softly.

The standoff becomes silent for an excruciating length of time. Everyone is breathing heavily. No one dares to move. Suddenly, Paolo spins and points the gun at Adamo.

"Adamo, shoot me!"

Everyone is startled by Paolo's words. Adamo is surprised and sweating profusely.

"No. Don't make me."

"Shoot or I'll splatter your brains."

"We don't have to do this."

Paolo begins shaking as if having a seizure. His eyes look about erratically. He's sobbing. He and Adamo are staring at each other. Everyone else is motionless. Paolo takes a slight step backwards, then a few more. He slinks out like a deadly cheetah who has lost his prey. Adamo starts to follow. Renzo commands otherwise.

"No, let him go. There is no purpose in killing him. Sorrow will be his executioner."

Ozzie Logozzo

PART TWELVE

"The first cut is the deepest." – Rod Stewart

Chapter 47

Tarquinia, Italy

"*Buongiorno, professor* Renzo. You are up early this morning. *Che Dio ti benedica* (God bless you)," says the woman looking down from her balcony.

I look up from my refreshing drink of water at the *fontana monumentale di piazza Matteotti*. I'm waiting for Anna-Maria to exit the municipal building. She's in conference with Sebastiano detailing the funding for the new construction of a schoolhouse for elementary kids. It feels strangely comfortable to be addressed as *Professore*.

"*Buongiorno, signora. Grazie mille* (Many thanks)."

A frail oriental woman is nursing her flower

pots on a second-floor balcony while a young woman, Emma, who flashes me a smile, is opening the security iron gates to the variety store below. The building is on the opposite corner to the *carabinieri* station house which was previously my schoolhouse when I was a child.

"My bones are calling for rain today. Shouldn't you carry an umbrella, Professore?" asks the elderly woman.

'*Professore*' is a formality used throughout Italy to address someone of elite standing.

"*Grazie*. I have one in the car," I smile.

Vatican Bank money has been used to renovate the monumental fountain which displays the coat of arms of Pope Innocent II Conti, the Roman cardinal of *Corneto (Tarquinia)*. I remember, as a boy, running around the circular marble bath like a tightening spiral spring inside a clockwork toy and then releasing my stored energy with a sprint through the city streets, homeward bound. Its central column, surmounted by a cross, has been central to my life. Everything about this place feels like a saline solution to my soul.

I see Adamo in front of the station house resting against the trunk of a police car directly in front of the entrance to the church. He smokes marijuana for pleasure and to relieve ailments, both imagined and actual. The balcony lady gives Adamo a look of disapproval before reentering her home. The young woman storekeeper lingers outside, spying him coquettishly.

I approach Adamo.

"You realize that she likes you a whole lot,

right?" I ask.

"Indeed, she does. As much as her mother disrespects me."

"Make the daughter happy and the mother will learn to love you as well," I say.

Adamo gives me a self-conscious glance. I think I've scratched the surface of what could be a promising romance. I'm ecstatic. I give him a friendly punch to his upper arm.

"Good for you. She'd be lucky to have you," I say.

Adamo aims to divert the dialogue.

"I got word that Ali has yet to return to her university post in Toronto. Perhaps, she's still here in Italy?" says Adamo.

"Perhaps," I reply without interest before asserting, "Here comes Anna-Maria."

Anna-Maria is descending the exterior steps of the municipal building to the right of the arched alcove that houses a park bench. Two old men look on in admiration. Attired in a fitted black skirt and blazer overtop a white buttoned-up shirt she walks proudly across the cobblestone street, perfectly balanced on her high-heeled pumps. She smiles and waves at me. As I wave back, I glimpse a woman retreat backward under the shadow of the arched passageway just right of the *Tabacchi* store.

I'm jabbed by the onset of recognition. Is it an illusion? An impression brought on by long suppressed feelings? I try to dismiss the sensation as Anna-Maria approaches and greets me with a kiss the cheek, but the emotion returns as does an unexplainable sense of guilt.

"Sebastiano assures that the schoolhouse construction will begin within two weeks. Our next stop is Rome. Pope Virgilio is expecting us for brunch," says Anna-Maria.

I open the back door to the *carabinieri* sedan for Anna-Maria as Adamo slips into the driver seat just after blowing a surreptitious kiss to his sweetheart. Once again, I spot movement in the shadow across the *piazza*. It's not an illusion...but it's not logical either.

I slide into the backseat along with Anna-Maria who locks her arm around mine. The warmth of her body and the sweet smell of her perfume is soothing. I void my mind of petty uncertainties.

"If you two want to make out in the backseat, go ahead. I'll turn on the siren so I can't hear a thing," smiles Adamo.

Unnerved, Anna-Maria giggles.

"Ooh, I like that idea," coos Anna-Maria.

I blush like a virginal adolescent.

Adamo maneuvers the vehicle out of the *piazza* around the fountain and turns to travel down the hill toward the entrance to the old town and outward to connect to the highway to Rome. As we pass the arch I'm stunned by a figure that's stepping farther back into the shadowy cocoon.

I see her clearly. It's no illusion. Emily has returned to *Tarquinia*.